The Ten Cupcake Romance

M.L. Kennedy

SCHOLASTIC INC.
New York Toronto London Auckland Sydney

ISBN 0-590-33932-X

Copyright © 1986 by M. L. Kennedy. All rights reserved. Published by Scholastic Inc.

12 11 10 9 8 7 6 5 4 3 2 1   5   6 7 8 9/8 0 1/9

The Ten Cupcake Romance

A Wildfire® Book

WILDFIRE® TITLES FROM SCHOLASTIC

I'm Christy by Maud Johnson
Dreams Can Come True by Jane Claypool Miner
An April Love Story by Caroline B. Cooney
Yours Truly, Love Janie by Ann Reit
Take Care of My Girl by Carol Stanley
Nancy & Nick by Caroline B. Cooney
Senior Class by Jane Claypool Miner
Junior Prom by Patricia Aks
He Loves Me Not by Caroline Cooney
Good-bye, Pretty One by Lucille S. Warner
Christy's Choice by Maud Johnson
The Wrong Boy by Carol Stanley
The Boy for Me by Jane Claypool Miner
Phone Calls by Ann Reit
Just You and Me by Ann Martin
Holly in Love by Caroline B. Cooney
Spring Love by Jennifer Sarasin
Little Lies by Audrey Johnson
Broken Dreams by Susan Mendonca
Love Games by Deborah Aydt
Miss Perfect by Jill Ross Klevin
On Your Toes by Terry Morris
Christy's Love by Maud Johnson
Nice Girls Don't by Caroline B. Cooney
Christy's Senior Year by Maud Johnson
Kiss and Tell by Helen Cavanagh
The Boy Next Door by Vicky Martin
Angel by Helen Cavanagh
Out of Bounds by Eileen Hehl
Senior Dreams Can Come True by Jane Claypool Miner
Loving That O'Connor Boy by Diane Hoh
Love Signs by M. L. Kennedy
My Summer Love by Elisabeth Ogilvie
Once Upon a Kiss by Susan Mendonca
Kisses for Sale by Judith Enderle
Crazy Crush by Stephanie Gordon Tessler
The Boy Barrier by Jesse DuKore
The Yes Girl by Kathryn Makris
Love to the Rescue by Deborah Kent
Senior Prom by Patricia Aks
Dating Blues by Maud Johnson
Brian's Girl by Diane Hoh
A Girl Named Summer by Julie Garwood
Recipe for Romance by Terri Fields
The Ten Cupcake Romance by Mary Lou Kennedy

One

"It's happened again," I said breathlessly to my best friend, Sharon Blakely. "I've fallen in love for the twenty-third time. This year!"

Sharon, a cool blonde with cornflower blue eyes, regarded me calmly. "So it's cupcakes this time, is it?" she said, sweeping my room with her icy gaze. She sighed and began counting wrappers. "One, two, three, four. . . ." She reached under my bed and gathered up the rest of the crushed wads of cellophane. "Ten!" She looked at me incredulously. "This could be serious, Amy."

"It is," I whispered. "This time it's the real thing, Sharon. I just know it! I've just met the most fantastic boy in the whole world." I sank down happily on my waterbed, and hugged a zebra-striped throw cushion to my chest.

"For your sake, I certainly hope so,"

Sharon said. She looked at my Saturday morning outfit suspiciously, and I wished I had taken the time to find a belt for my oversized sailcloth blouse.

I'm five-seven with green eyes; naturally wavy, brown shoulder-length hair; and an okay figure. Sharon says that if I would lose six pounds I could be a model, but I'm just not into clothes the way she is.

She looked sensational, as usual, in a canary yellow sweater with brown and black tweed pants. Both her parents are psychologists and are very big on the "dress-for-success" look.

"Honestly, Amy, I don't know how many more of these crushes your waistline can take." She plunked herself down on the waterbed next to me, causing a small tidal wave.

"They're not crushes," I said indignantly. "Don't you believe in love at first sight?"

"I suppose so," she said thoughtfully. "But with you, it happens every five minutes." She smiled. "Well, let's hear about your latest. I suppose he's different from every boy you've ever met."

"Absolutely." I grinned, remembering some of Sam's one-liners. "Okay, his name's Sam Collins and he's really funny, for one thing. I've never met anyone who can make me laugh the way he does — "

"Sure you have. Andy Cranshaw. Last summer," Sharon said promptly. "You were in love for fifteen days straight and ruined your teeth with six pounds of black jelly beans."

I stared at her. Sometimes it's a bore to have a friend with a steel-trap mind. "Sam's very intelligent," I stammered. "He scored over seven hundred and fifty on the SAT — "

"So did Scott Faircloth," she said pointedly. "On the math portion." She shuddered delicately. "I'll never forgive him for causing you to pop that grape bubble gum in my ear night and day." She paused and picked at a thread on her sweater. "Although I have to admit it was a change after Jerry Mendel. Remember when we drove all over town looking for strawberry licorice ropes? Just because he didn't call for one whole weekend!"

"Okay, enough!" I pleaded. "You know that when I'm in love, I tend to overeat a little."

Sharon stared at me. "A little?" She raised her eyebrows meaningfully.

I shrugged. Sharon never lets you get away with anything. "All right, a lot," I admitted. "Look, Sharon, your parents are psychologists. You know that people react differently to being in love."

"That's true," she agreed. "Some people write poetry, and pace the floor all night, some *forget* to eat and waste away to nothing. . . ."

"And . . ." I prompted her.

"And some people pig-out on junk food," she said flatly. Not what I wanted to hear at all. "Look, Amy," she said, consulting her watch, "it's eleven-thirty on a Saturday morning. I don't want to sound heartless, but I really don't think this latest crush will last more than forty-eight hours."

"Forty-eight hours?" I said, smiling.

"That's right," she said confidently. "In just forty-eight hours, you and Sam will be" — she made a shape in the air like a mushroom cloud — "pouf! Over, kaput, finished. You'll realize that he's not, and never will be, your one and only."

"And why do you say that?" I was still smiling.

She sighed and stood up, pressing an imaginary crease out of her pants. "Because Sam Collins, the love of your life, invited me to have lunch with him at eleven-thirty Monday morning. And that's just forty-eight hours from now."

"What!" I squealed, jumping to my feet. "The rat! Wait till I get my hands on him!"

"Easy, Amy," Sharon said, resting her hands lightly on my shoulders. "You're acting out — "

"I'm what?"

"You're acting out, behaving aggressively. And it's not a very smart way to deal with your problem. It's self-destructive. It will only make things worse." She gave me a sweet, patient smile, exactly like Dr. Joyce Brothers.

"What should I do?" I said weakly. I felt suddenly deflated. In the space of a few minutes my world had turned upside down. Not only had Sam Collins dumped me for my best friend — and worse, had invited her to lunch, which is my favorite meal of the day — but I learned I was a bundle of confused aggression. What else could go wrong?

Sharon was saying something, and I forced myself to pay attention. "There are some excellent books on the subject," she said earnestly. "Books that help you get over unhappy love affairs," she added, reading my blank expression. "I'll get my parents to recommend one. In fact, I'll even buy it for you."

"That's very nice of you," I muttered. Sharon was probably right. It was time to get over all these crushes. Being a prisoner of love has its drawbacks, I thought, remembering the thirty boxes of cupcakes I had stashed under the bed. Who would eat them now?

"That's okay," she said airily. "You can count it as an early birthday present, or an early Christmas present."

I tried not to smile. My birthday was six months away, Christmas was three. Of course, that wouldn't bother Sharon, who is one of the most practical persons I know.

"I'll bring it to school on Monday, okay? We can go over it together at lunchtime." She wound a black silk scarf around her neck and double-knotted it in the back. I sucked in my stomach, and wished I had tucked in my shirttails. It's easy to feel like a bag lady next to Sharon.

"Then you're not going to lunch with Sam?" I said quietly.

"Go to lunch with Sam Collins?" She looked at me incredulously. "Of course not. I turned him down flat. Not my type at all." She paused and looked at me. *Not anybody's type,* her eyes said.

"Amy," she said slowly, "can I give you a piece of advice?"

"Can I stop you?" I giggled nervously. "No seriously, go ahead," I invited.

She picked up the hem of my sailcloth blouse with her long lacquered nails, sighed, and let it flop limply against my jeans.

"Do me a favor and wear a belt with this. Please." She gave me a dazzling smile and made a fast exit.

"What's a peanut butter and banana sandwich doing in the middle of the shag rug?" my mother demanded early Monday morning.

Waking-up is never the best time of day for me, but I smiled, surprised that my mother was into riddles. I yawned and turned over. "I give up," I said pleasantly. "What's a peanut butter and banana sandwich doing in the middle of the shag rug?"

"That's what I'm asking you," she said, her voice rising to a dangerous squeak. I peeked out of the covers, and saw my mother pointing to a brownish mess next to the bed.

"Gosh," I said quickly. "I don't know how that got there." Actually, I knew very well.

6

I had made a midnight snack the night before, carried it into my room, and munched on it in bed while my mind raced over Sam Collins' betrayal. I must have fallen asleep. . . .

"Well, how about cleaning it up?" she said, exasperated. "I'm already late for work."

"Sure," I said, jumping out of bed. I made a hasty trip to the bathroom and took a stab at the rug with a wet Kleenex. It wasn't a tremendous success. If I hadn't been daydreaming about Sam Collins, this never would have happened, I thought, annoyed with myself.

My mother watched me thoughtfully from the doorway. "Is something wrong, Amy?" she said searchingly. "You've been in a world of your own lately. Nothing's wrong at school is it?"

"No, not at school." I hesitated. "I got some bad news this weekend, though. I . . . uh . . . got dumped by a boy," I told her, trying for a smile.

"Oh no," she said, her face softening. "And Chuck was such a nice young man. . . ."

Chuck? Who was Chuck?

"Of course, you know what they say about summer romances," she went on dreamily. "When fall comes, they're as dead as a faded suntan."

As dead as a faded suntan? My mother has a knack for choosing strange similes. She went downstairs then, and it finally dawned on me. She was talking about Chuck Nelson, a lifeguard who I had briefly dated in August. Chuck Nelson! My mind raced back to a boy with sandy hair and an unlimited supply of white shorts and pale blue T-shirts. Chuck Nelson, a bronzed god with the IQ of a houseplant. I giggled, wondering how I ever could have been attracted to him. Then I remembered something, and sobered up fast. Chuck Nelson was — I counted rapidly — at least fourteen boys ago. Fourteen boys since last August!

Sharon was right. I needed help.

"Here's the book," Sharon said excitedly a few hours later. She plunked her tray down and slid into a seat next to me. "I'm glad you saved us one of the little tables. The last thing we need today is people eavesdropping on us."

"Right," I said, staring at her plate. Sharon is one of those lucky people who could eat like a horse and not gain an ounce. Today her plate was piled high with a mock Thanksgiving dinner, complete with turkey and cranberry sauce.

"Well, aren't you going to open it?" she said impatiently.

I looked down at the paper bag she had thrust into my hands. "Of course, I just . . . Sharon, did you get stuffing *and* potatoes?"

She stared at me and frowned. "Amy, is food the only thing you ever think about?"

Hah! She should know the answer to that one.

"No," I said, embarrassed. "But I just can't figure it out. How come you can eat the special every day, while I'm stuck with the diet delight?" I pointed to my lunch, which looked more unappealing than ever. The waxy pear had a faintly green tinge to it under the fluorescent lights, and the cottage cheese was a little watery. I poked it with my fork. Definitely watery.

"I told you," she said patiently. "It's all in your mind. Calories, weight, everything. If you think thin, you'll be thin," she added firmly. I tried not to watch as she tucked into a pile of sweet potatoes topped with marshmallows and walnuts.

"Hmmm, maybe you're right," I said absently. I began flipping through the book she'd bought me. *How To Mend a Broken Heart* was the title. I liked the cover immediately. A bright red heart with a heavy silver zipper running down the middle. "Cute," I said, grinning.

"It's more than cute," Sharon said seriously. She leaned toward me confidentially. "It works. My mother used it on a patient who had suffered through fifteen unhappy love affairs."

Fifteen. Maybe there was hope for me after all. "What happened to her?" I asked, curious.

"Well, I'm not supposed to discuss the

specifics of any case," she said importantly, "but. . . ."

"But?"

Sharon lowered her voice to a whisper. "She *married* the sixteenth." I waited. "He was a dentist, and they moved to Omaha, Nebraska, last month."

"Oh," I said. Sharon frowned. She obviously wanted more of a reaction than *that*. "That's very nice," I amended.

"People's whole lives have been changed by this book," Sharon said softly. "It's got a very tough approach."

"It does?" I turned to the first chapter and saw what she meant. "How to get the jerk out of your life for good," I read aloud.

"That's right." She laughed shortly. "In just six easy steps." She stabbed her mashed potatoes and gravy. "In fact, I think we better get started right away. I hate to say it, but the object of your affections is heading this way."

Oh no. It was Sam Collins, weaving his way across the lunchroom with that lazy smile I remembered all too well.

"Be strong," Sharon hissed.

I nodded. I didn't feel strong. For some stupid, insane reason, my stomach was doing flips and my mouth was dry. I was a nervous wreck.

Sam looked gorgeous. It wasn't enough that he had curly dark hair and choir-boy eyes like Paul McCartney. Today, of all days, he had to wear a brown leather bomber's jacket over an Irish knit sweater. I reminded myself that he had dumped me for Sharon, and resolved not to throw myself at his feet.

When he got to the table, he grinned, first at Sharon, then at me. "Hi ya."

"Hello," Sharon said cooly, and kicked me under the table.

I managed to find my voice. "Hi, Sam." I tried for a casual tone, but I don't think he was fooled for a minute. Boys can spot adoration a mile away, and he probably knew that I couldn't take my eyes off him.

"Too bad it's a table for two," he said huskily. He stood in the aisle balancing his tray.

"Too bad," Sharon murmured. She shot me a look.

"We're almost finished," I piped up. "You could have our table if you like."

Sharon kicked me again. "No, we're not," she said sweetly. "Pumpkin pie is part of the special, and I'm going back to get some in a minute. Anyway, you haven't finished your cottage cheese, Amy," she pointed out. She stared at the droopy mass on my plate.

Sam took the hint. "Well," he hesitated, "guess I better find a seat before my lasagna melts. Maybe I'll see you guys later." He smiled and moved toward a table full of giggling cheerleaders.

"Well, now," Sharon said brightly, "that wasn't so bad, was it?"

"It was awful," I said glumly. "I'm still crazy over him, I can't help it." I heard a high-pitched squeal from somewhere behind me, and resisted the urge to look over my shoulder. Sam Collins had struck again.

"Amy Miller, what am I going to do with you! Didn't you see the way he acted just now? He practically ignored you, plus if you remember, he asked me out to lunch today. Not you. He's a first-class rat." She sipped her iced tea. "Doesn't that bother you at all?"

"I've got a very forgiving nature."

She sighed and pushed away her empty plate. "You better start chapter one while I get my dessert. I can see you're going to be a real challenge, Amy."

I watched as Sharon made her way back to the cafeteria line. She hesitated, and then carefully put two pieces of pumpkin pie with whipped cream — and two forks — on her tray.

I smiled and ducked back to my book. So Dr. Freud had a heart, after all.

Two

By an almost superhuman effort, I managed to avoid Sam Collins for the next few hours. "Out of sight, out of mind," was one of the key rules in *How To Mend a Broken Heart*, and I intended to follow the advice to the letter.

This meant I had to avoid all my usual routes in school. I knew Sam's schedule as well as I knew my own, and normally I managed to "accidentally" bump into him half a dozen times a day.

I was skulking along a basement corridor after a particularly deadly geometry class, when suddenly my blood ran cold. Sam Collins, looking fantastic in navy blue shorts and a white T-shirt, popped out of the boys' locker room, just a few feet ahead of me. I caught myself admiring those muscular legs and impossibly broad shoulders and knew I had to get away — fast. But where? My heart thumping like a rabbit's, I rounded a corner at breakneck speed and nearly collided with Oscar Carson.

Oscar Carson looks exactly like Alfred E. Neumann, the carrot-topped nerd from *Mad Magazine*, and the two of us have never hit it off. In fact, the truth is this: I hate him more than fried liver. He's loud, obnoxious, and never misses a chance to make a sarcastic remark or put someone down.

When he saw me hurtling past him in a mad rush, he behaved in typical Oscar Carson fashion. He flashed me an evil grin and stuck out his foot. It was the old story of the irresistible force and the unmovable object. There was a long, slow-motion sequence when my books went flying against the wall, my purse emptied its contents on the dirty linoleum floor, and I landed in an ungraceful heap by a trash bin. Behind me, I heard Oscar's hysterical chuckle.

Like a cat, I had managed to get my feet under me when I fell, and I scrambled up gingerly, wondering if I had any broken bones. I whirled around furiously, but Oscar was strolling down the corridor, whistling tunelessly, probably looking for new victims.

I was brushing off my skirt when I heard a low male voice behind me.

"I saw what that creep did. You should really put him on report, you know."

Only one person in our entire school says things like "put him on report," and I turned to grin at Simon Adams, a new student who'd moved to our town from England. Simon is a nice-looking boy who always talks like he's just escaped from *Masterpiece Theatre*. Mrs. Fitzsimmons, my drama teacher, nearly faints every time Simon opens his mouth, and she calls on him twice as often as the rest of us. In fact, she made him read the whole first act of *Julius Caesar* in class last week, and he had to play all the main characters. Simon is pretty good-natured about things like that. As he says, it could have been worse; we could have been studying *Romeo and Juliet*.

"What's the use," I sighed. "Everybody knows what Oscar is like. This just isn't my day," I muttered.

"Problems?" Simon said sympathetically.

"Like you wouldn't believe," I began and then choked on my words. What was I doing! In another minute, I'd be blubbering all over his Izod shirt, blurting out the whole sad tale of Sam Collins and his irresistible blue eyes. "It's nothing you want to hear about," I said hurriedly.

"But I do." Simon's voice was low and husky, and for a crazy moment, I felt like confiding in him. Then the bell rang, and sanity took over.

"I've got to stop at my locker before French," I said quickly, and left at a gallop. I left Simon standing in the middle of the hall looking bewildered, but what else could

I do? Anyway, I reasoned, the last thing I needed right now was to get involved in a conversation with a boy — any boy.

"How's it going?" Sharon whispered a few minutes later. She shot a nervous look at Madame Trennant, who was writing some irregular verb conjugations on the board. I waited a moment before answering. Madame Trennant has an uncanny knack for knowing when someone's talking or passing notes. She must have eyes in the back of her head, because she can whip around in a flash, and zap you with twenty pages of translation.

"It's going pretty well," I whispered back. Actually, I was very proud of myself. I had only thought of Sam Collins forty-seven times between homeroom and French.

"Really?" she said dubiously. "I didn't expect the book to work this soon. You only read a few pages."

"Well, it's a start," I explained. "I still have a long way to go, but I'm on the right track. In just a few days, Sam Collins will be — " I frowned, trying to remember what my mother had said. "As faded as last year's suntan."

Sharon gave me a puzzled smile. I guess she couldn't figure out my mother's similes either.

By the middle of the hour, I was suffering withdrawal symptoms. It was exactly as if Sam Collins was a drug I was addicted to!

I finally gave up and let my mind wander, knowing where it was headed. . . .

Sam and I were walking hand-in-hand along a sandy beach on a blisteringly hot day. I was wearing a pale blue bikini and my hair was blowing in the wind, just like someone in a shampoo commercial. The beach was nearly deserted and a few gulls were circling lazily overhead.

After a few minutes, Sam and I stopped walking and stood staring into each other's eyes. "Amy," he whispered, touching me gently on the cheek. A delicious shiver went through me, as his suntanned arm slid around my waist. Would he kiss me? I waited, my toes tingling from the icy whitecaps breaking against the shoreline.

"Amy," he repeated softly. "I think I love you." I closed my eyes, knowing that in the next few seconds, his lips would meet mine in a warm, wonderful kiss.

"I love you, too," I started to say, but was suddenly cut off by a stabbing pain in my ribs. I gasped, my eyes flew open, and I was aware of a lot of things happening at once. The images tumbled crazily through my mind, like a film run on fast forward. Sharon Blakely pulling her hand back from my rib cage. The big oak clock over the blackboard with the hands permanently stuck at two-thirty. The curious stares of the kids in the next aisle. Somebody snickering in the back of the room.

And worst of all, a shadow looming over me. No, it wasn't a shadow; it was Madame Trennant.

"Amy, are you with us yet?"

How long had she been standing there?

I wanted to die. I wanted the gray linoleum floor to open and swallow me up. I wanted to vanish in a puff of smoke or melt into a puddle of wax. Unfortunately, none of these things happened, and I had to face Madame Trennant, who was tapping a ruler in her hand.

"Earth to Amy," she said with a thin smile.

"Uh, yes, Madame," I stammered.

"If you've finally decided to rejoin us, Amy, perhaps you'd like to translate paragraph sixteen."

"Uh. . . ."

I looked desperately at the opened book on my desk. I was on the wrong page, of course. How long had I been daydreaming?

Sharon reached over and quickly flipped forward a few pages. She tapped her fingernail on paragraph sixteen, and gave me a meaningful look. The rest was up to me.

I stumbled through the translation, with my cheeks flaming. The moment the bell rang, I scooped up my books and darted out of class. Sharon was too quick for me, though, and caught up with me in the hall.

"I knew it! You were daydreaming about Sam Collins again, weren't you? I thought you said you were cured," she said accusingly.

"I didn't say I was cured, I said I was on the road to recovery. There's a difference, you know."

"I'll say!" she sniffed. "If I were you, I'd get started on chapter two the minute you get home." She buttoned up her tomato-red wool jacket, and flipped her long blonde hair over the collar. "I'll call you around nine-thirty tonight for a progress report," she said grimly. "And remember what Laura Chambers said."

"Laura Chambers?" I asked stupidly.

Sharon rolled her eyes. "The author of *How To Mend a Broken Heart.*" She paused dramatically. "She said: 'If you can't get him out of your head, you'll never get him out of your heart.'"

"I'll remember that," I promised. I smiled, hoping I looked a lot more confident than I felt.

"If you can't get him out of your head, you'll never get him out of your heart." I was standing at the sink a couple of hours later, repeating the words over and over to myself.

"Talking to yourself?" my brother Matthew said wryly. I nearly jumped out of my skin.

Matthew's seventeen, a star basketball player, and moves quietly, like a panther. He strolled over to the refrigerator, poured himself an enormous glass of milk, and grinned at me. It was the grin that did it. Whenever Matthew smiles that way, I know that it's not going to be my day.

"What have I forgotten?" I said wearily.

"Funny you should ask," he chortled. He pointed to the wall calendar. "Today's your day for dinner," he said calmly.

"What!" I shrieked. "It can't be!"

"See for yourself," he said, easing his six-foot-two frame into a kitchen chair. "Whose book is this?" he said curiously, fingering my copy of *How To Mend a Broken Heart*.

I ignored him, and stared in horror at the calendar. A few months ago, my mother read a book on time management and announced she was going to "restructure our home environment."

At first, Matthew and I thought it was just a joke, but slowly, the awful truth set in. From that day on, Matthew and I would be expected to cook dinner on weeknights, do our own laundry and ironing, and generally provide slave labor for the household.

I glanced at the clock. Five-thirty! My only hope was to defrost something quickly. I yanked open the freezer door, and minutes later, a mound of tinfoil was soaking in a pan of hot water.

"Interesting," my mother said thoughtfully, taking a bite of shredded chicken. "What is it?"

"It's a recipe we learned in home ec," I said earnestly. "Chinese . . . um, spicy chicken."

"Why's it so stringy?" Matthew said with a devilish smile.

I glared at him, but he avoided my eyes, pretending to push his vegetables around on his plate. Half an hour earlier, he had watched as I cold-bloodedly crammed three frozen chicken breasts in the blender. The chicken was successfully "shredded," even though the blender had screeched like the Concorde and had finally gone into cardiac arrest. A quick trip to the frying pan, half a jar of duck sauce and presto — instant Chinese dinner.

"You're a fine cook, Amy," my father said absently. Actually, I don't think he ever notices what he's eating. Dad's a systems analyst for a big computer firm and his mind is usually miles away on one of his projects. Mom said that when she first met him, she thought he was very dreamy and romantic. Whenever she'd talk to him, he'd listen quietly with this funny half smile on his face, never saying a word. She thought he was enchanted by her.

It was several months before she realized he looked at everyone that way. He wasn't enchanted at all! When he gets that faraway look on his face, it usually means he's wrestling with a graphics display problem or working on a new way to do sequential analysis.

It was nearly seven by the time I escaped to my room. I grabbed the Laura Chambers book and sprawled on the waterbed, eager to find the "path to contentment." According to the author, all I had to do was take control of my life and passions, and happiness would follow. It would be a snap!

By eight o'clock, I had my doubts. Laura Chambers' ideas were unusual, to say the least. In fact, they sounded crazy! Chapter two explained all about love and hate. "Love and hate are flip sides of the same coin," I read. "If you love someone, you're just inches away from hating him." I read that line twice, and still didn't understand it.

I didn't hate Sam Collins! I was crazy over him. That was the whole problem.

I decided to try one of the exercises in chapter three. I was supposed to draw a line down a sheet of notebook paper, and make two columns, A and B. Column A would list all Sam's good points, and column B his bad points. "When you've finished," Laura Chambers said cheerily, "you'll find that his bad points far outweigh his good ones! You'll begin to wonder what you ever saw in him. . . ."

Except it didn't work out that way. When the phone rang at nine-thirty, I had covered three sheets of paper and was still working on column A. I loved everything about Sam Collins. He didn't *have* any bad points that I could see.

"How's the prisoner of love?" Sharon said dryly.

I explained about columns A and B.

"Don't be silly," she said briskly. "I can think of one glaring fault he has."

"What's that?"

"He doesn't love you back."

True. She had stumped me on that one. I was trying to muster a bright comeback when she cut me off.

"Have you come to the part about the cold spaghetti?" she said enthusiastically. "It's my favorite part of the whole book."

"Cold spaghetti?"

"I think it's in chapter five. Every time you catch yourself daydreaming about your boyfriend, you're supposed to imagine him covered in wet, slimy spaghetti." She laughed happily. "Isn't that a scream?"

"What's the point of it?" I asked, puzzled.

"Honestly, Amy, don't you understand anything about psychology? That's the perfect way to cure any romantic fantasies you have about this guy."

"I suppose I could give it a try," I said doubtfully. "It sounds a little bizarre, though."

"Bizarre!" she snorted. "It's a well-known therapy technique. My mother said so." She paused. "You *do* want to get over him, don't you?"

I thought of the incident in French class. "Of course I do! If wet spaghetti is what it takes, then bring on the Parmesan," I said grimly.

"That's the spirit," Sharon said encouragingly. "Just remember, tons of soggy pasta trailing down his face . . . tomato sauce splattered all over him." She gave a fiendish chuckle.

I was beginning to wonder if Sharon was *enjoying* all this.

Three

"You look like you just escaped from *The Village of the Damned*," Sharon said calmly the next morning. Sharon's a horror movie freak, and probably set a Guinness Book record when she sat through *The Bride of Dracula* fourteen times.

I peered at myself in the girls' room mirror and groaned. I had to admit that I looked a little paler than usual. My green eyes were sunken, and lined with heavy dark circles like Cleopatra's. Except I hadn't painted them with Egyptian kohl, I'd lain awake half the night thinking about Sam Collins.

"I'm not at my best today," I said lamely.

"Not at your best!" She started to laugh and then stopped when she saw a couple of seniors watching us curiously. "Being in love is ruining your looks," she hissed. "It's about time that you pull yourself together, Amy Miller." She lowered her voice to a whisper.

25

"By the way, have you seen you-know-who today?"

She meant Sam Collins. "Not yet. But I've come prepared." I pointed to a bright red rubber band I was wearing like a bracelet. "Chapter six," I explained. "Whenever I catch myself thinking of him, I have to snap it against my wrist. By the end of the day, I'll probably be rubbed raw." I laughed a little nervously.

"Let's hope not," Sharon said cooly. "After all, the whole key to self-discipline is — " The buzzer sounded just then, and she made a face, grabbing her books off the sink. "Darn! I've got a history test this period, but I'll call you after school. And remember," she added warningly, "when you see Sam Collins, think spaghetti. You got that? Cold, wet spaghetti!"

"Got it," I said weakly.

"And don't forget this. You need all the help you can get." She reached over and snapped the rubber band once, painfully, before she darted out the door.

I rubbed my wrist and stared in the mirror. It wouldn't hurt to get in a little practice before my big moment. "Cold wet spaghetti," I whispered. "Trailing down his face . . . looped over his ears . . . tomato sauce splashed on his nose and a big, juicy meatball — "

I heard a faint snickering behind me and stopped abruptly. The two seniors had put down their hairbrushes, and were staring at me, open-mouthed.

"Uh, just rehearsing," I said weakly. "School play," I tried a smile that didn't quite make it and waltzed out the door.

"Looks like you're planning on some heavy studying," Sam Collins said to me half an hour later. I was tottering out of the library with a load of books when he suddenly materialized next to me. The moment of truth! I could feel his warm breath on my cheek as he peered over my shoulder, and predictably, I lost the power of speech.

"I've got some . . . reports due," I warbled.

"Uh, huh," he said politely. He smiled at me and waited. *Now what!*

"We're studying Faulkner and Hemingway this semester," I babbled on, wishing I could tear my eyes off his dark brown hair and shoulders. It's funny, I thought, I never noticed what an unusual color his eyes are, or the way they're fringed with those thick black lashes. . . .

Suddenly Sharon's face floated into my mind like an evil genie, and I took a deep breath. It was time to "think spaghetti."

Sam was saying something about his English class, but I wasn't really listening, because I was squinting my eyes and doing my best to picture him covered in pasta. Piles of slimy spaghetti draped over his forehead. . . .

He brushed a stray lock of hair out of his

eyes and I could feel myself weakening. It didn't matter if Sam was covered with wet spaghetti — he looked adorable, no matter what! I thought of Sharon and tried again. Trick strands of fettucine looped over his ears . . . tomato sauce dribbling down his nose. . . .

I almost had the picture locked in my mind, when he suddenly leaned close to say something. That was my downfall. I could smell the faint tang of the citrusy aftershave he wore, and my heart started beating like a tom-tom.

It was obvious that I hadn't made any progress at all; I was as hung up on him as ever. Should I give it one last shot? I stared hard at his right ear, and tried to imagine it covered with marinara sauce. There was just one problem. He didn't look silly or disgusting, the way the book promised. He looked . . . fantastic. I had a wild impulse to wipe away the imaginary marinara sauce and kiss his ear. I sighed and gave up.

Two things crossed my mind: one: I was doomed to be hopelessly in love with Sam Collins for the rest of my life; two: Sharon Blakely would kill me.

At the moment, I didn't know which was worse.

The phone was ringing when I got in the door after school, and I didn't have to be a psychic to figure out who was calling.

"Hello, Sharon," I said quietly.

For once, she was caught off guard. "How'd you know it was me?" she asked.

"A lucky guess." I dumped my books on the kitchen table and reached for a chocolate chip cookie.

"Any success today?"

I took a deep breath and told her about the spaghetti experiment. "It just didn't work," I said miserably. "Maybe nothing will. . . ."

"What about the rubber band trick?"

I hesitated. There are some things you don't even want to tell your best friend. "I discovered I have a high tolerance for pain. I snapped the rubber band so many times, my wrist started bleeding and Mrs. Roberts sent me to the nurse."

There was a long pause while I munched thoughtfully on another cookie. "So unless you have some other brilliant ideas, I'm afraid this is it."

"I think it's time to call in the experts," she said slowly.

"The experts?"

"My parents. After all, they deal with this kind of thing all the time."

"You mean you want me to see them — as a patient?" I was horrified.

"No, nothing that formal." She laughed. "Why don't you come over for dinner tonight? We can talk about your problem and see what they suggest. It's worth a try."

"Well okay," I said hesitantly.

"It's been so long since we've seen you, Ali," Sharon's mother told me over the appetizer.

"Amy," Sharon corrected her patiently.

I practically drooled, inhaling the aroma of the thick Parmesan crust on the bubbling onion soup. So far, so good. A definite improvement over the tuna fish number.

"We always try to keep up with Sharon's friends, but honestly, one gets so busy nowadays, it's simply *fou*."

Fou. We learned that in French class. It means mad or crazy, which seemed like a strange choice of words for a psychologist to use.

"But it's nice that you were able to join us tonight," she said, reaching over and patting my hand. "Sharon has told us what a great friend you are. She says you are *tres sympathique*." She flashed me a bright smile, and I grinned back. Actually, I like Dr. Blakely. But she has an annoying habit of scattering French words through the conversation like bread crumbs.

"Sharon tells us you have a bit of a problem," her father, the other Dr. Blakely, said.

"Well, I don't know if you'd call it a problem," I hedged.

"Of course you would," Sharon interjected. "Classic obsessive-compulsive syndrome. Right out of the textbook." She gave a smug smile.

"Sharon, please," I said weakly. At times, she's about as subtle as a bulldozer.

"And the source of this obsession. . . ." Dr. Blakely let his voice trail off, and all three of them peered at me.

"A boy," Sharon said promptly. "At the moment it's Sam Collins, but it could be any boy. Isn't that right, Amy?" Without waiting for a reply, she rushed on. "Amy gets these mad crushes on boys and then goes through weeks and weeks of agony trying to get over them. She's a love junkie."

"Now, wait a minute," I protested. I tried to sound indignant, but it was hard with a mouthful of gummy cheese.

"How many times have you been in love?" Sharon persisted.

"Twenty-three," I muttered.

"Ah-hah! What did I tell you? An emotional yo-yo," Sharon said solemnly. I was beginning to get annoyed. Sharon meant well, but in another twenty years, she'd sound exactly like her mother.

"Hmmm," Sharon's mother said knowingly. "She probably has thin boundaries." *Thin boundaries?* "Have you tried the Laura Chambers book, dear?"

"Yes, I finished it last night," I stammered.

"It didn't work," Sharon said darkly. Her eyes strayed to my wrist, and I hastily dropped my hand in my lap before she could say anything.

"Sharon tells me you've tried avoidance therapy," her father said gently.

"The rubber band didn't do a thing," Sharon asserted. "I think if she was zapped with a mild electric shock every time she thought about him — "

"I don't think that will be necessary," he interjected quietly. "Amy, I think I've got an idea that might help you. People with thin boundaries tend to be very creative," he began.

I nodded, and tried to look interested.

"They're open to life, and relationships. . . . They don't have the defenses that the rest of us have built up." He stopped and smiled encouragingly at me. "You know, there's a way you could use your experience to your own advantage. It would be creative, and it would be very good therapy." He paused and toyed with a fork. "You can put your own broken heart to work for you."

"I can?" I said, intrigued.

"You can. Have you ever thought of writing a book?"

"Writing a book?" I tried not to laugh. I didn't even keep a diary.

"A book! That's a wonderful idea, Charles," Sharon's mother bubbled. "Amy, it would be so . . . cathartic. You'd get all your feelings out in the open — "

"But what kind of book could I write?" I interrupted.

"A love story, what else?" Sharon said

excitedly. "You should write a romance novel!"

"I wouldn't know where to start," I began.

"Begin with yourself, silly. It's not like you have to run to the library and do research."

"Not if you've been in love twenty-three times," her mother said gently.

"I suppose you're right," I said, getting excited over the idea. Maybe it wasn't so crazy, after all.

"I'll think about it," I promised.

"It sure beats snapping rubber bands," Sharon teased.

"You've got a point." I looked around the table at their smiling faces and suddenly felt wonderful. "I'm beginning to think there's hope for me, after all."

F^{our}

"I can't believe my parents came up with such a great idea," Sharon said happily after dinner. "You're going to be a romance writer! It's a fantastic solution. I don't know why we didn't think of it ourselves." She smiled and sprawled on the tan and white plaid studio couch she uses for a bed. I bypassed a Scandinavian "backless chair" and looked for a comfortable place to sit. Sharon's room is ultra-modern, and filled with enough chrome and steel to outfit a dentist's office. I finally settled down in a black leather number that could tilt in eighteen different positions — perfect if you were having root canal work done.

"Well, first things first," Sharon said, reaching for her note pad. "Okay, what time frame did you have in mind?"

"Time frame?"

"You know, the Civil War would be a great

setting," she said thoughtfully. "Think of the costumes — all those bonnets and bustles, and the men get to wear great-looking uniforms. And there's lots of opportunity for tragedy . . . the hero could be a brave soldier who gets killed in the last chapter. Or better yet, a general." She made a note, and then frowned. "No, wait, we better scratch that. He can be wounded, but not killed. Romance books always end happily, don't they?" She started to write furiously and then looked up. "Do you think he should be a Rebel or a Yankee?" she asked suddenly.

A Rebel or a Yankee? Sometimes it's hard to keep up with the strange twists that Sharon's mind takes. "Sharon, what are you talking about?" I pushed a button on the armrest, and my legs flipped up helplessly in the air.

"Your book," she said patiently. "I thought we'd start to outline it tonight. You know, sketch in the settings, the characters, maybe do a little work on the plot. . . ."

I stared at her and she flushed. "Look, Amy, I don't want you to think I'm taking over or anything like that." She tapped her pencil nervously against the pad. "But, if you'd like, I could be your collaborator." She gave me a shy smile. "I mean, if that's okay with you."

"My collaborator?"

"You'd do the actual writing," she explained, "but I could give you suggestions. I could be sort of a sounding board for your ideas. Plus, I have a few of my own," she added modestly.

It only took me three seconds to make up my mind. "It's a deal," I said gratefully. "Two heads are better than one, and you seem to know a lot more about this than I do." I was having trouble thinking with my legs jutting out at right angles to my body. And I was beginning to realize that I had no idea at all how to write a novel. I even have trouble composing thank-you letters.

"I guess I hadn't thought about setting the book in the past," I said hesitantly. "You really think I should?"

"Oh, definitely," she said earnestly. "Historical romances are very popular right now. And you wouldn't have to use the United States, if you didn't want to. A lot of them are set in England and Scotland." She sighed and tucked her legs under her. "The romantic possibilities are endless . . . dark mansions, windy moors, heroines wandering around shivering in long velvet capes."

I didn't think it sounded very romantic, and started to say so. "Sharon, I really don't — "

"In fact . . . how would you feel about the hero wearing a kilt?" she asked very seriously. "It could be very effective, on the right sort of boy."

A kilt! I nearly burst out laughing, but caught myself just in time and shook my head. There was no sense in antagonizing my collaborator before we even got started.

"Okay, no kilt." She made another note and chewed the end of her pencil thoughtfully. "I'm afraid we're back to square one. We still haven't settled on the time and place."

"There are so many possibilities, I don't know where to start," I said dazedly. I was feeling dizzy, probably from all the blood rushing to my head.

"Maybe we should start with the hero first. Who are you going to model him after?"

"I don't know," I said weakly, knowing I was out of my depth.

"C'mon," Sharon said impatiently. "That's the whole reason you're doing the book, remember? To get all these guys out of your system, once and for all. Just think back to the boys you've dated. Who was the most exciting? Who would be the perfect romantic hero?"

"Gosh, it's hard to say," I said. I pressed another button and was almost ejected onto Sharon's glass-top table. I rubbed my shin gingerly and tried to think. "I liked different boys for different reasons. They all were special in one way or another," I said helplessly.

"Even Chester Newton?" Sharon said dryly.

"Especially Chester Newton." I smiled, remembering a lank-haired nerd with a calculator strapped to his belt.

"I never could understand what you saw in him," she said thoughtfully.

"Uh, he kind of . . . grew on you," I said, avoiding her eyes. I didn't want to admit that Chester had done my algebra homework for me for an entire semester and I had gotten a B-plus in the course. Whoever said that love is blind must have dated Chester Newton.

$F^{\underline{ive}}$

"How's it going?" Sharon said brightly the next morning. We were jostling for a spot in front of the girls' room mirror, just as the first period bell was about to ring.

"Not so hot," I admitted, scrambling in my purse for a comb. "I can't even make up my mind about the locale — "

She stared at me and burst out laughing. "I'm not talking about the book, silly. I meant your wild crush on Sam Collins."

Sam Collins! Unbelievably, I hadn't even given him a thought for . . . almost fifteen hours. Sharon read my expression and sighed. "How fickle you are," she murmured teasingly. "Just think, a couple of days ago, you were in the depths of despair because he was ignoring you. And now. . . ." She let her voice trail off meaningfully.

"I'm still in the depths of despair," I said indignantly. "At least I would be, if I just had more time to think about it," I amended. "Sharon," I said, trying to stifle an enormous yawn, "do you know that I was up till two this morning, trying to come up with a plot?"

"You were?"

"I was." I thought it best not to mention that I was still struggling with my vision of the perfect romantic hero, too. Should he be blond or dark-haired? Athletic or intellectual? Funny or serious? I had absolutely no idea.

She stopped brushing her already perfect hair and looked at me. "I thought you'd have made some kind of a rough outline by now," she said with just a hint of reproach. "In fact, I was kind of hoping we could start work on the first chapter this weekend."

"I was hoping for that, too." I shrugged unhappily. "Writing a book is a lot tougher than I thought it would be."

"You're not going to give up on the idea, are you?" she said, as the bell rang. "Because I picked up a few things at the bookstore for you — "

"No, of course I'm not giving up," I said hurriedly. "I just think I need some expert advice." I glanced down at my English lit. book and suddenly got an idea. "And I think I know how to get it," I told her.

"But Amy — "

"See you at lunch," I promised. "I'll explain everything then." I ignored the surprised look on her face and darted out the door.

* * *

Mrs. Harding's eyes widened in surprise when I poked my head in her tiny office and told her I was going to be a novelist.

"Amy, that's wonderful," she said enthusiastically. "Come in and sit down," she urged me with a big smile. Her office was so cluttered it looked like she was holding a paper sale.

"I hate to bother you," I began apologetically, "but I really need some advice."

"Don't be silly, it's no bother," she assured me, beaming. "You know, Amy, I had no idea you were so interested in writing. Not that your work in class hasn't been, uh, promising," she added quickly. "Now, I want you to sit down and tell me all about it," she offered, sweeping a pile of term papers off a chair. "That is, unless you're on your way to class?"

"No, I've got a study hall this hour," I assured her. I sat down gingerly on a wobbly folding chair and stared across the desk at her. I've always liked Mrs. Harding, even if I don't share her passion for English. She's been teaching literature at Andover High School for at least twenty years, and she loves her subject. Her idea of a really terrific weekend, she told me once, is to take the phone off the hook, and curl up with the complete works of Charles Dickens.

"Now," she said briskly, "how did all this come about? What made you decide to write a book?"

I hadn't thought she'd hit me with a zinger right off the bat. "I just thought it would be fun to try something different," I said slowly. I hated to fib, but I could hardly tell her that I was the victim of twenty-three crushes, and was trying to break out of my "prison of love"!

Mrs. Harding looked at me so seriously, I had to choke back a giggle. "You decided to try something different," she repeated. A strand of silver-streaked hair escaped from her neat chignon, and she pushed it back impatiently.

"Yes," I went on, wondering if I sounded believable. "I've had this . . . idea . . . bouncing around in my head for weeks now, and I just wanted to put it down on paper."

"And you decided to write a novel," she said, bemused. "Well, I suppose a lot of writers start out that way," she said, smiling. "An idea gets hold of them and just won't let go."

"That's it exactly," I said, grinning at her. If only she knew how close to the truth that was! Sam Collins was holding onto my heart like a persistent terrier and the book was my only chance to shake him free.

"And how can I help you?" she said.

"I'm having trouble getting started — "

"Ah, writer's block," she said sympathetically.

"Something like that." I paused and stared at the rows of books lining the walls: English and American novels, mostly, with

French poetry taking up the row beneath them. "I remember once you said in class that a novelist has to create a whole world and set it in motion," I began.

"That's right. And the hard part is knowing when to start the world, and when to stop it."

"Hmm." I nodded, wondering what to say next.

"It would help if I knew what kind of novel you had in mind, Amy," she said, sensing my hesitation. "Is it a mystery book, or an historical — "

"It's a romance novel," I blurted out. I could feel the heat rushing to my cheeks. "It's got to be."

She raised her eyebrows questioningly, and I felt like ripping out my tongue. "I mean, it doesn't *have* to be, but I've always wanted to write a love story, Mrs. Harding." If I was Pinocchio, I thought guiltily, my nose would have grown three feet by now.

"A love story," she said softly. "Well, you're in good company, Amy. Some of the world's greatest writers have turned their pens to love," she added, staring out the window. "Of course, in many cases, it's unrequited love . . . makes for better fiction," she added with a chuckle.

"Unrequited?"

She nodded. "That's what happens when the person you're in love with doesn't love you back."

"I can certainly relate to that," I muttered.

Now I had a name for what was wrong with me — I was suffering from unrequited love. "That's exactly the kind of book I want to write," I said firmly.

"Then let's find a way to break that block," she said kindly, and headed for the shelves. "How about a little inspiration from the classics? It never hurts to see what other people have written, you know. Sometimes that gives you just the spark you need to get started on your own project."

She squinted over the titles for several minutes while I waited. "I think you'll find these helpful," she said, finally, handing me a pile of dusty hardbacks. "They may seem a bit heavy going at first, but stick with them. After you've read them, we can talk about them, if you like."

I glanced at the titles. *"Anna Karenina, Madame Bovary . . . Romeo and Juliet?"* I said questioningly.

"The greatest love story of all," she said with a smile. "Even if it ended in a tragedy."

I took the books and sighed, wondering if they really were going to help. "Thanks," I told her, glancing at my watch. I said a silent prayer that Sharon had enough sense to save a table in the lunchroom for us; we had a lot to talk about.

"You will let me know how your project is going, won't you, Amy? In fact, maybe you would consider reading a little of your work in class and letting us discuss it. You never know, it might encourage other students to become authors. . . ."

I smiled. "As soon as I get something down on paper, you'll be the first to know," I promised her.

"I thought you'd never get here!" Sharon said irritably. "I've only got a few minutes to eat, because I've got to go to the library before history class." She handed me a tray, and after glancing at the special — tuna delight — we headed for the salad bar.

She waited until we were settled at a corner table before handing me a shopping bag from the Book Nook. "You can consider this a very early Ground Hog's Day present." she quipped. "It's something to help you get on the right track."

I pulled out three shiny new paperbacks and whistled in surprise. They were all popular romance novels, and I couldn't help but grin at the titles. *"Love's Sweet Slave?"* I giggled. The girl on the cover had long red hair down to her waist, and was locked in a passionate embrace with a cavalry officer. Apparently Sharon was still on her Civil War kick.

"It's on the best-seller list this week," Sharon said stiffly. "And the cashier said that the other two were their most-requested books."

I picked up the second and shook my head in amazement. It was a Gothic romance and pictured a girl with flowing black tresses riding a giant white horse in the moonlight. In the background was a grim-looking mansion set high on a cliff. "Hmm, very dramatic," I muttered. " 'Constance Carmichael . . . only a few dared to know her true identity.' " I read aloud. " 'What secret was she hiding beneath her ebony velvet cape?' "

"She's a highwayman," Sharon explained eagerly. "I read a few pages while I was waiting for you."

"Highwayperson," I corrected her automatically.

Sharon ignored me and speared an olive. "She's actually the daughter of an earl, but she robs carriages at night to avenge the honor of her brother."

"He's a highwayperson, too?" I couldn't believe Sharon was taking this so seriously.

"No, of course not," she snapped. "But an evil duke stole her brother's dagger and used it to murder the mayor of Bainbridge on All-Hallows Eve —"

"You got all that out of a few pages?" I interrupted.

"Well, you kept me waiting for ten minutes," she said, jutting her chin out the way she always does when she's annoyed. "Besides, the book moves very fast. We should probably make a note of that for our novel," she said, whipping out her notebook. "Keep up a fast pace," she muttered to herself, scribbling across the page.

"I'll try to remember that," I said dryly.

How had "my" novel suddenly become "our" novel, I wondered? I pulled out the third book, and winced.

"Love on the Range?" I said questioningly. Apparently, I had saved the worst for last. A girl in a flame-colored dress and high heels was smiling at a rugged-looking cowboy wiping his face with a bandanna. "What's this one all about?"

"They meet at a dude ranch. She's an account executive for a big New York advertising company, and she's looking for a cowboy to star in a television commercial — "

"Don't tell me," I laughed. "I can guess. She hires him for the job, he makes a fortune, and they ride off happily into the sunset together."

"Really, Amy," she said disgustedly, "if you're going to make jokes about everything. . . . Those books cost me almost six-fifty."

"I'm sorry," I said contritely. "It's just that everybody is giving me books to read, first Mrs. Harding, and now you. You should have seen what Mrs. Harding recommended — *Anna Karenina, Madame Bovary. . . .*"

"Humph!" Sharon snorted. "A Russian who throws herself under a train, and a bored housewife who poisons herself."

I was silent for a moment, and Sharon decided to renew her attack. "Look, Amy," she said haughtily, "you admitted you've done zilch on the book, and apparently you're no great shakes in the plot department. So what's wrong with taking a look at books like these? It never hurts to see what other people are doing."

"That's what Mrs. Harding said," I told her. "It's just that the two of you have such . . . different ideas of what a romance novel should be like."

Sharon sighed and crumpled up her napkin on her tray. "Well, this is what sells at the Book Nook, Amy, so I'd read them carefully if I were you. And don't be so quick to make fun of them. *Love's Sweet Slave* has sold over two million copies!"

"I'll keep an open mind," I promised her. Secretly, I just couldn't get excited over books about highwaypersons and cowpokes. Still, if they were selling over two million copies, somebody must be reading them. . . . I thought of Sharon's cracks about Mrs. Harding's selections. She thought they were out-of-date, boring. But *Anna Karenina* and *Madame Bovary* have been around for over a hundred years. So the question was: Who was right?

I was sitting pondering the problem long after Sharon had disappeared to the library, when a masculine voice broke in on my thoughts.

"I didn't know that was your style," Simon Adams said, sliding into the seat next to me.

"My style?" I said stupidly.

"You just don't seem the type for Gothic

romances." He pointed to Constance Carmichael on her trusty steed. "You're not reading it for class, are you?"

"No," I said, and then flushed when I realized he was kidding. "It's not even my book," I improvised quickly. "These all belong to Sharon. She was in such a hurry to get to the library, she forgot them." My second fib of the day. "So, what are you up to?" I said, desperate to change the subject.

Simon smiled, a really nice smile that showed off his even white teeth. "Well, I thought you might have a minute to go over our French assignment with me. But I don't want to interrupt your lunch," he said.

I pushed the remains of my wilted salad aside. "That's okay. Endive isn't something you want to linger over. What did you want to know?" I asked, flipping open my battered copy of *French for You and Me*.

"I missed that class when she went over the imperfect tense," he began. "Maybe you could help me do some of these translations. . . ."

I was listening politely, filling in the right verbs for Simon, when all of a sudden, my heart gave a giant lurch. Sam Collins was standing just a few feet away, pushing his tray halfheartedly through the cafeteria line. He looks gorgeous, even from the back, I thought unhappily. Light blue shirt, tan chinos, broad shoulders, and a narrow waist. . . .

I flinched when Simon nudged me. "Amy," he said, a puzzled look in his eyes, "We're on number ten. . . ."

"Right," I said, dragging my attention back to the book. I sneaked another look at Sam and was rewarded with a view of his profile, as he moved forward in the line. He even has adorable ears, I mused. There was something unbelievably attractive about the way his dark hair curled over his ear lobe.

He was making a joke to a pretty blonde next to him, and the sound of her laughter floated across the room. Darn it all, I still had a crush on him. It just wasn't fair! But there was no sense in wishing things were different between us. It was better to take a philosophical attitude. The Blakelys had said something like that over dinner.

"If it could have been, it would have been," I said softly. I didn't even know I had spoken aloud until I saw Simon's bewildered expression.

"What number are you on?" he said, scanning the page.

"Sorry, I just got ahead of myself," I apologized. "We're right here," I said, stabbing the page with my finger. Out of the corner of my eye, I saw Sam and the blonde heading for a table at the far end of the room. Out of sight out of mind? Maybe. But for how long. . . ?

Six

In the end, it was my mother who came up with the perfect solution to my problem. I was sprawled on my waterbed before dinner, still wrestling with plot ideas, when she wandered in with a mug of steaming cappuccino.

"Studying hard?" she said with a smile.

"No, actually I . . ." I hesitated. Maybe it was better to tell the truth and get it over with. "I'm writing a book."

My mother has what Sharon's mother would call *sangfroid*, which means a bomb could go off under her nose and she wouldn't even flinch. So I wasn't surprised when she looked at me calmly and sipped her cappuccino before murmuring, "A school project, I suppose?"

"Nope," I said, grinning. "It's just for fun."

"Fun?" she repeated quizzically. "You're writing a book for fun?"

"Sure," I answered, trying to make a joke of it. "You've written tons of ad copy and travel brochures. Haven't you ever been tempted to put all your thoughts and feelings down in a novel?"

She smiled and gave a little shudder. "I'd rather have my fingernails pulled out. One by one." She sat down in my desk chair and tucked her feet under her. "Well, tell me more about this book of yours. What's it about?" I caught her staring at the paperbacks strewn all over the bed, and wished I'd stuffed them back in the shopping bag.

"It's about love," I said with a straight face. "You know, romance."

"Sounds interesting," she said, with a little smile playing around her mouth. "This doesn't have anything to do with Chuck, does it?"

She was still thinking of Chuck, my lifeguard from last summer. "Oh no, it's not about him," I hedged. "In fact, I don't even have a main character yet. The truth is, I'm kind of stuck." I told her about Sharon and Mrs. Harding, and waited while she thumbed through the books they'd given me.

"Nineteenth-century novels and modern romances," she said slowly. She gave me a very direct look with her cool gray eyes. "I think I see what the problem is, Amy. You can't get started with your own writing, because neither one of these styles is quite right for you."

"They aren't?" I was relieved, because I had come to exactly the same conclusion.

"No, not at all. The books Mrs. Harding gave you are classics, but they're much too sophisticated for you — it would be impossible to copy them. And as for the ones Sharon bought you. . . ." She let her voice trail off and gave an eloquent shrug. "Well, they're a little remote from your own experience, don't you think?" She stacked the books in a neat pile on the desk. "If I were you, I'd forget all about these, and start over — from scratch." She looked at me very seriously, the steam from her cappuccino rising in wispy threads around her face.

"But where do I start?" I said helplessly.

"Start with your own experience, that's the obvious place. Forget about dude ranches and lady thieves. Why not write about what it's like to be a high school girl and fall in love? You'll be able to borrow from everybody you know — from Sharon, and from all the rest of your friends and classmates." She drained her cup and got up. "But don't overlook yourself. The best books are autobiographical, anyway, I always think."

"I hadn't thought of writing about myself." But it would be a lot easier than writing about a female Robin Hood, I decided, remembering Constance Carmichael and her white horse.

"Why not?" She laughed. "It's one subject you should know a lot about."

"I guess you're right," I agreed. "Maybe I've been making this too complicated."

"I'm sure you have. After all," she added, "there must be a thousand kids at Andover High. . . ."

"And that means a thousand different stories," I said, feeling a little shiver of excitement go through me. "You know something? I think it would work, I really do!"

Matthew popped his head in the door just then, and flashed a martyr's smile. "Mom, do you think you could bone the chicken for me? It's got all this yuckky stuff inside," he said piteously. "And the butcher left the *skin* on it."

"You never bone it when it's my night to cook," I objected.

Mom's got a soft spot for Matthew and she smiled apologetically. "Now, honey, you know Matthew's got a weak stomach," she began. "It really bothers him to see food in its raw state. He such a sensitive boy."

A weak stomach? Matthew was the only kid in advanced biology who could dissect a squid and eat lunch on the same day.

The moment Mom disappeared toward the kitchen, Matthew grinned idiotically and made an okay sign at me. I threw *Love's Sweet Slave* at him, but it was only a half-hearted gesture. I was much too excited by Mom's suggestion to be really angry with anyone. It was suddenly all so simple. I'd use my own experiences and write a book that high school kids would want to read over and over. In its own way, it would be a classic.

The heroine would be bright, intelligent, attractive — after all, Mom did say it should be autobiographical. And the hero would be modeled after. . . .

My mind skidded to a halt. I couldn't model him after Sam Collins! I was still in the throes of my crush, and it was taking every bit of strength I had not to throw myself limply at his feet. I knew I'd never get over him if I had to think about him, and write about him, every single day.

No, the hero should be someone else. Someone I knew casually, who I wasn't the least bit attracted to. After all, everyone knows that a writer must be objective. So the whole trick was to pick someone I wasn't, and would never be, in love with.

I felt a wave of relief wash over me, but it was short-lived. It sounded so easy, but who would I pick? I sat there for another half hour and all I came up with was a giant question mark.

Fate has a way of stepping in at the oddest times. I was reading my French book in the library the next day, yawning over the adventures of a pair of boring twins called Paul and Marie Duval, when Simon Adams slid into the seat across from me.

I looked up, smiled briefly, and went back to the Duval twins, who were having a riotous time picking grapes in the south of France. It didn't take much to make them happy, I thought idly.

"Hi," he said brightly. He was staring at me in a funny way, and made no move to open his book.

"Hi, Simon." I stretched and turned to the questions at the end of the section. Madame Trennant always made us answer them — *en français*, of course — at the beginning of class. It was a sneaky, but effective, way of finding out who had and who hadn't read the chapter.

"I didn't get a chance to do the assignment today," he said, still looking at me intently. "I had soccer practice till eight last night, and well, you know how it is. . . ."

I wondered why he was confiding in me, but said lightly, "Well, you didn't miss much, believe me. Paul and Marie are spending a vacation in the south of France."

"I spent a holiday there last year with my family," Simon piped up. "It was fabulous. We went to the Grand Prix in Monaco, and then hung around for the film festival in Cannes. They're doing the same sort of thing, I suppose."

I laughed out loud, and Mrs. Harris, the librarian, shot me a dirty look. "Not quite, Simon," I said, in a low voice. "Paul and Marie are living in a tent and picking grapes in a little hill town above Antibes. They call it a working vacation."

"Oh." He grinned at me. "Not much of a

holiday, is it?" He paused, and I noticed he looked more British than usual in a heavy chocolate-brown sweater that matched his eyes. "Say, would you mind if I took a look at a few pages? I don't want Madame to catch me off guard."

"Don't you have a book?" I started to say, but he was already on his way around the table toward the empty seat next to me.

"Lost it," he said casually, pushing his chair very close to mine. "Why don't you give me a quick rundown on what the Terrible Twosome is up to this week?" he added, flashing me a winning smile.

"The Terrible Twosome — is that what you call them?" I said, starting to giggle. "I always think of them as the Dreadful Duo, myself." I flipped back a few pages. "Okay, here we go. Paul and Marie are visiting many wonderful sights on the Riviera...." I translated quickly.

"I thought you said they were living in a tent," he interjected.

"They don't stay in the tent all the time, silly. On their days off, they take the bus into Nice and go sightseeing. See, it says so right here." I pointed to a paragraph, and Simon must have pointed at the same time, because suddenly his hand closed over mine. It was an accident, of course, and we both drew our hands back, embarrassed.

"So they pick grapes all week, and go into town on weekends. Fascinating." He turned the full force of his brown eyes on me.

"Knowing those two, they probably visit a raisin factory."

I laughed out loud again, earning another murderous look from Mrs. Harris. "If you keep making jokes, she's going to throw us out of here," I whispered.

Then he did a really surprising thing. He reached over and tapped me on the nose! "Only if you keep laughing at them," he corrected me solemnly.

I stared at him for a minute, not sure what was going on. Simon was acting different, somehow. I'd known him since he came to Andover last year, but he was looking at me today like he'd never seen me before. And his arm . . . was I imagining it, or had he purposely let it trail over the back of my chair? Another half inch and it would look like he had his arm around me. I almost giggled again, just thinking what Mrs. Harris would have to say about that!

"I really need a tutor, you know," he was saying seriously. "I just can't get the hang of French the way you do."

"Madame Trennant has a list of some seniors who do tutoring," I suggested. I was smiling at Simon, but keeping one eye warily on Mrs. Harris, who looked ready to descend on us like a hawk.

"Yeah, I know that." He paused and inched his chair a little closer. "But they wouldn't take a personal interest, would they?"

"Probably not, but — " I stopped abruptly,

with my jaw hanging open. Could Simon possibly be hinting around that I be his tutor? And — even crazier — was he interested in me as more than a tutor? It seemed strange but all the evidence was there. Even as I hesitated, I could feel his hand graze the back of my blouse ever so gently. He pretended he was just shifting his position in his chair, but I knew better.

Unless I was sadly mistaken — and I'm usually right about these things — Simon Adams was making a play for me!

"I can't believe it," Sharon said flatly later that afternoon.

"Thanks a lot," I told her, and finished off the dregs of a double chocolate ice cream soda. We were sitting in a red vinyl booth in the back of the Ice Cream Factory discussing strategy for the book, when I told her about my encounter with Simon.

Sharon took a delicate sip of her strawberry malt and looked at me speculatively. "I just meant he's not your usual type," she said smoothly.

"Sharon," I reminded her, "I've been in love twenty-three times. Everybody's my type."

"True," she laughed. "I suppose if Count Dracula wandered in here right now, you'd ask him what he was doing Saturday night."

"Very funny." I took a last sip and was rewarded with a loud slurping noise. Sharon raised her eyebrows disapprovingly, but I ignored her and rushed on. "Anyway, I can always tell when a boy is interested in me, and believe me, Simon's interested." Even as I said it, I felt a little rush of pride. Simon Adams, while not my "type," as Sharon said, was a very attractive boy. In fact, it was just a sheer accident that I hadn't formed a mad attachment to him by now, I decided.

If this was a cartoon, a light bulb would have suddenly flashed over my head. The idea hit me with such force that I nearly knocked over my empty glass. "That's it!" I said aloud. "Simon Adams will be my hero. I don't know why I didn't think of it before," I said, shaking my head.

Sharon was looking at me as if I had lost my mind. "Are you going to let me in on the joke?"

"It's no joke. Simon is going to be the boy of my dreams, the love of my life. Not in real life," I said quickly. "In the book!"

She gave me a blank stare, and I remembered that I hadn't told her about my mother's suggestion the night before. As far as Sharon knew, I was all set to write a sequel to the Constance Carmichael book. As patiently as I could, I outlined my mother's ideas.

"So you see," I finished, "Mom thinks I'll do better if I stick to my own experiences, and not go too far afield."

"I don't think *Love's Sweet Slave* was that far afield," she said huffily. "And *Love on the*

Range was certainly . . ." she paused, groping for a word ". . . topical."

"No, they were wonderful books," I hastened to reassure her. "And I really appreciate them. But I just don't think I could do them justice, Sharon. Remember how Mrs. Harding always says we should write about what we know? Well, that's what I want to do." I looked around the crowded restaurant. "And this is what I know. High school kids. Going to school, falling in love — "

"Getting over crushes," she said, smiling.

I nodded. "Their ups and downs, their successes and disappointments. . . ." I felt excited, sure I was on the right track at last.

"No windy moors or mansions?" she said a little sadly.

"Not this time."

"No royalty, I suppose."

I laughed. "Not unless Simon's related to an earl."

"So you're definitely going to use Simon Adams as the main character."

"He's going to be the love interest, as they say." I paused. "Whatever Simon says and does is going to end up in my book." I wished I had my note pad with me, because I wanted to jot down something about the way he had rested his arm on the back of my chair earlier that day. And the way his dark eyes were so piercing and direct. His voice was unusual, too, I decided, deep and husky, just right for a romantic hero. . . .

She thought for a moment. "Amy," she

said slowly. "I hate to burst your bubble, but did it ever occur to you that Simon may not feel like being raw material for a novel? You say you think he's interested in you. Fine, you may be right. But what makes you think he's going to want his thoughts and feelings captured on paper for everyone to see? I bet you never thought of that," she added smugly.

"Oh, I thought of it," I grinned. "And I also figured out the perfect solution." I paused for effect. "I'm not going to tell him."

Seven

I woke up the next morning full of energy. By the time the sun was creeping through the blinds and snaking across my paisley bedspread I was showered and dressed, eager to start the new day.

Every day, at seven sharp, my mother opens my door and says exactly the same thing: "Rise and shine, honey." This time was different. She took one look, staggered back in surprise, and gasped: "You're up!" Her tone made it clear that I had performed an amazing, and nearly impossible feat. My mother isn't a morning person, and makes no secret of the fact that she's never seen a sunrise in her life.

"Of course I'm up," I said, smiling.

She sank down on my bed, cradling a cup of coffee, and peered at me. "And you're dressed to kill," she added, covering a yawn. "Is something special going on today?"

I certainly hope so, I felt like shouting, but I restrained myself. "Nothing much," I told her, adding a touch of lip gloss. I wasn't really dressed up. I had just taken a little more care than usual, choosing a new ruffly white blouse, a tan macrame belt that was a gift from Sharon, and my very best jeans.

"How come you're wearing makeup?" she added. "It's not the day for school pictures, is it?"

"No," I laughed. My mother knows that unlike Sharon, whose makeup kit is the size of a small suitcase, I'm strictly a soap and water person.

But today I had experimented with some dark brown eye liner, a smudge of pearly blue shadow and a couple of layers of mascara. I had to admit I liked the effect. But would Simon? I wondered silently. I had to make an impression on him, I thought, my stomach turning over lightly. I had to make him want to ask me out. . . .

The buzzer on the microwave went off, and my mother wearily got to her feet. "Well, you certainly look very put together for an ordinary day," she told me. Then she smiled at me over her shoulder. "But I like it."

Of course, my mother had no way of knowing that it wasn't an ordinary day. It was the first day of my new career, my new identity. I looked in the mirror and grinned at a face that would someday appear on book jackets all over the world. Amy Miller, romance novelist.

* * *

My first inkling of trouble came before math class that morning when Lucy Skinner corralled me in the hall. Lucy is a tall, bony girl with red hair and zillions of freckles. She's on the girls' basketball team, and she has an unfortunate habit of punctuating her statements with a sharp jab to her listener's shoulders. A few minutes with Lucy, and you wander away looking like a bruised banana.

"Sharon told me you're writing a book," she said in a voice that could shatter glass.

"She did?" I said, looking nervously up and down the corridor. How many other people knew? What if word drifted back to Simon? The whole project could be killed before it even got started!

"She shouldn't have done that," I complained.

"Look, I know it's supposed to be a secret," Lucy said, lowering her voice to a husky roar. "But Sharon said you were interested in using some real-life experiences, and well . . ." she ran a hand through her carrot-colored hair ". . . let's just say I've had my share of romances."

"You have?" I said and immediately realized it was the wrong thing to say. As far as I knew, Lucy enjoyed a rich fantasy life, but that was all. I'd never seen her out with a boy, and she had caused a minor sensation last year when she attended the Junior Prom with her parents, who were acting as chaperones. I could still remember her in her pink taffeta dress, hanging around the punch bowl, staring at the dancing couples like a lovesick flamingo.

"Does that surprise you?" she asked coldly.

"No, of course not," I protested hastily. After her Junior Prom caper, *nothing* would surprise me. "And I really appreciate your wanting to help me, but the thing is . . . well, all this is supposed to be confidential."

"I know that," she said sharply. She raised her hand to jab me in the right shoulder, but I deftly turned, so all she caught was the edge of my notebook. "After all, I wouldn't tell my romantic experiences to just anyone, you understand. I mean, Sharon practically begged me for material, and you know how persuasive she can be."

"Yes, I certainly do," I said, managing a light laugh. I could hardly wait to see Sharon so I could strangle her.

"And she told me everything would be in the strictest confidence, and that you'd change the names around so no one would know who your sources were."

"Oh, absolutely," I promised her. Of course I'd change the names around. Did she really think I'd write a romance book about a girl who had never had a date?

"So what do you say we have lunch together, and I'll go over some of the details with you? You can take notes," she said generously. I saw her hand coming up again and I ducked, but too late.

"That would be . . . fine," I said, gingerly

rubbing my shoulder. "Just you and me and Sharon."

She looked surprised. "Oh, didn't Sharon tell you? Karen Clover and Shirley Hill have tons of experiences they want to share with you." She laughed slyly. "You're going to have so much material you won't know what to do with it. It looks like all of Andover High is ready to kiss and tell." She chortled like she had just said something terribly wicked.

"Ha, ha. It sure seems that way," I said, inwardly seething. I couldn't believe it. Sharon, my so-called collaborator, had told practically the whole junior class about my book! My only hope was to find Simon and get the ball rolling before he suspected anything. I checked my watch. Maybe I could catch him before French class.

"Hi," I said cheerily.

"Hi, Amy." Simon returned my greeting, a little surprised.

"I thought we could walk to French together," I went on, as casually as I could. The trouble was, it's hard to sound casual when your chest is heaving, and your lungs feel like they're going to explode.

"You seem a little out of breath," Simon said, in what had to be the understatement of the year.

"Out of breath? Oh no." I tried to laugh merrily, but instead I made a croak like a dying frog. I had spotted Simon crossing the quad a few minutes earlier, and had been sprinting like Mary Decker to overtake him.

"In fact, I've never felt better." He looked unconvinced, and I heard myself rambling on. "I've been doing a lot of jogging lately," I said in a burst of invention.

"Really? That's great. Maybe we can run together sometime," he said smoothly.

Run together! My carefully rehearsed speech fell apart, and I scrambled to make a quick recovery.

"Sure," I said, trying to sneak a few breaths. "Simon, I just thought of something . . ." I began. I closed my eyes, feeling a wave of dizziness wash over me. At this rate I'd never get the chance to write the first line of a novel — I'd have a heart attack right at Simon's feet.

"Yes?" he said seriously, turning the full power of his brown eyes on me.

"Well, I know you said you were having trouble with verb declensions in French. . . ." I paused, wondering if he'd fall for it. "And I thought maybe you'd like to drop by my house this weekend to study with me." I held my breath, and pretended to be absorbed in a stray piece of wire on my spiral notebook. I twisted it back and forth until I got it into place, avoiding his eyes.

"I'd like that very much." *He fell for it!*

"That's great," I said, grateful that my pulse was returning to normal. "We can study together whenever you want. I wouldn't want to interfere with your week-end plans," I added coyly.

"Oh, you couldn't," he laughed, "because I don't have any. I've got a great idea, Amy. Why don't we spend Saturday together?"

"Together?" I echoed blankly. "You mean all day?" I blurted out, and could have kicked myself. Wasn't this what I wanted? It was the perfect opportunity to start my "romance" with him.

"Sure," he said enthusiastically. "It'll be fun. We can start with an early morning run, and maybe a bike ride through Ridley Park. Then a picnic lunch, and we'll study all afternoon."

Fun? It sounded like the decathlon! A run, picnic lunch, and some French study . . . that would take us up to about five o'clock, I thought, figuring rapidly. What was he going to do for the rest of the evening? He said he didn't have plans, but it sure sounded like he had a date, I decided, my spirits sinking.

"Of course the day doesn't have to end there," he went on, as if reading my thoughts. "There's a good movie playing at the Park. Or if you feel we haven't made enough headway in French by then, we can stick with that instead," he offered. "What-ever you want."

I smiled. "Okay, that sounds good to me." Actually, it would make wonderful material for the book. The picnic lunch could be very romantic — that is, if I survived the run —

and I had wanted to include a movie scene in the book anyway. Maybe we could even go out for pizza first. There would be a lot of colorful description in an Italian restaurant . . . red-checkered tablecloths, candles dripping rainbows of wax down musty wine bottles. . . .

Simon's voice snapped me back to attention. "Then it's on for Saturday?" he questioned, sounding very British.

"It's on all right," I told him. And how! I thought. The bell rang then, and we raced the few remaining feet to the main building, squeezing in the classroom door, just as Madame Trennant was about to shut it.

"*Bonjour, mes enfants,*" she said cooly.

"*Bonjour, Madame,*" we echoed. We slid into our seats, and Simon winked at me, as if we shared some wonderful joke.

I thought about the way I was planning to trick him, and felt a little guilty pang. He was so nice that I hated to lie to him, but what else could I do? If I told him I wanted to model a romantic hero on him, he'd never go along with the idea. And then my book would never be written.

No, I had to go through with the plan, I decided. It wouldn't hurt anybody, and someday Simon might even thank me. After all, how many boys are immortalized on paper? With that comforting thought, I opened my French book and gave my full attention to Paul and Marie.

* * *

"He asked you out for the whole day?" Sharon squealed when I met her in the cafeteria. "Amy, he must have it bad!"

"Well, he's definitely interested," I said modestly. I had intended to murder Sharon on sight for gossiping about my book, but I was so excited about my success with Simon that I decided to tackle the issue later. "I was surprised that he wants to spend so much time with me, but I guess it's a good sign. After all, the main thing is that he's taking me to lots of romantic places — "

" — to do lots of romantic things."

"All in the line of research," I said flatly.

"Oh, of course," she deadpanned.

She started to say something else but broke off suddenly when Karen Clover and Shirley Hill joined us.

"Hi, guys, we're just tossing around a few ideas." She shot me a worried look, and I knew she was wondering how I felt about my new "collaborators." It looked like everybody wanted to write my book for me!

"I heard that you two have some experiences you're just dying to share," I said sweetly.

"Yeah, we do," Karen said, dumping her tray next to mine. "Lucy was saying that you probably didn't have enough experience to write a romance book."

"Thanks a lot," I muttered under my breath. Sharon kicked me under the table, and I glared at her.

"So, we thought we'd help you out,"

Shirley said eagerly. She and Karen exchanged a look. "Do you want to start, or should I?"

"I'll start," Karen said flatly. "I remember the first time I knew I was in love. . . ." she began, and I let my mind wander. Karen was a large-boned girl with stringy blonde hair and a nasal voice. She had chosen the meat loaf special, I noticed, and I caught myself looking at it enviously. It's one of the few things that the cook at Andover knows how to make, and I was wondering if I could slip back and get some when Karen suddenly banged her glass on the table. "Honestly, Amy, shouldn't you be writing this all down? You'll never remember it."

Sharon gave me a sympathetic look, and I mumbled an apology. "Sorry, Karen, I was thinking of something else."

"Well, if you don't want my help, just say so," she said in a threatening tone.

"No, it's not that," I said hurriedly. "I was just thinking . . ." my mind went into overdrive as I groped for an excuse ". . .what beautiful hair you have. I was wondering exactly how to describe it." I peered dutifully at Karen's brassy locks, as if I were at a loss for words.

"What do you want to know about it?" she said grumpily.

"Well, it's hard to pin down the shade," I said tentatively. Actually, Karen's hair was multicolored, with dark roots, a blonde middle section, and bleached-out ends.

She pulled a strand in front of her nose and looked at it thoughtfully. "I'd say spun gold," she said flatly.

"Spun gold?" I repeated. I tried to keep a straight face as Sharon developed a terrible coughing fit and had to grab my Coke.

"Wouldn't you say so?" Karen demanded of Shirley.

"Oh, absolutely," Shirley parroted. "Spun gold."

"Now," Karen said, getting back to business, "if you have your notebook ready, I'll tell you all about Roger Erdman."

"Roger Erdman," I said, pulling out my pad and pencil like an ace reporter. "Who was he?"

"My first love," Karen said, heaving a great sigh. "Probably the only boy I ever *really* loved," she added, taking a giant bite of meat loaf. Being in love certainly hadn't hurt *her* appetite, I noted wryly.

"Only boy she ever loved," I wrote, wondering how I was going to use this in my book. Sharon was giving me a mischievous look from across the table, and I knew that she wasn't far from another fit of giggles.

I probed gently. "You and this Roger Erdman," I said quietly, "were in love. Did it end, uh, unhappily?" I sensed a tragedy lurking somewhere in the back of Karen's peroxided head.

"Did it ever!" she said, rolling her eyes to the ceiling.

"There was another girl?" I said, pressing for details.

She gave a sad smile. "No, I guess you could say it just wasn't meant to be." She paused for effect, watching me. "I was eight, and he was ten, when we met at a wienie roast at this summer camp up in the Adirondacks. We had a fantastic week together, but he lived in Minnesota, and I lived here in New York, so I knew there wouldn't be much of a future for us. Isn't that right, Shirley?" she demanded.

"Oh, absolutely," Shirley replied. "But Karen still talks about him," she said loyally.

"How touching," I said with gritted teeth. This was supposed to be material for a romance book? I looked at Sharon who was playing with her salad and refusing to meet my eyes.

I definitely had made a mistake with Sharon. I should have followed my instincts and murdered her before lunch.

E^{ight}

"Sharon, that was an utter waste of time,"
I muttered, when we were finally alone.
Karen had gone back for seconds on the meat
loaf, and Shirley was concocting something
fattening at the sundae bar. I was under-
standably jealous. So far, my lunch had con-
sisted of an untouched salad, and a massive
headache.

"Well, she was just trying to be helpful,"
Sharon said complacently. "Don't you think
you can use any of the material?" she asked,
looking at my notebook.

"I doubt it." I glanced at my spinach
salad — hopelessly soggy by now — and
pushed it aside. Every time I had tried to
take a bite, Karen had come up with another
fascinating detail about her love life, and insisted that I write it down immediately.

"Tell me about Simon," she urged. "I can't

believe you're going to spend the whole day together."

"I can't either," I admitted. "I dropped a huge hint about studying French together, and the next thing you know, he invited me jogging."

"I never thought it would be so easy," she sighed.

"It's not going to be easy, if he ever suspects that I'm writing a book," I told her. "I wish you had kept a lid on everything like you promised."

"I meant to, Amy, honestly, but we started talking about boys, and one thing led to another. Anyway, Simon won't suspect anything if you just play it cool — " She broke off suddenly and said quietly, "Uh oh, I just spotted the love of your life, three tables away."

"Simon?" I said puzzled.

"I should have said your former love," Sharon giggled. "Sam Collins."

"Oh, him." I said it so casually that Sharon looked at me in astonishment.

"Amy," she said wide-eyed, "you were madly in love with Sam just a couple of weeks ago. Doesn't it even bother you to see him?"

I looked over at Sam, who was surrounded by a table of adoring cheerleaders. The same dark hair, the same piercing eyes, and of course, that great smile with the flashing teeth. Everything about him was the same, and yet . . . different. I didn't feel the trembly excitement, the heart-stopping lurch I used to feel, and wondered why.

Sharon wondered the same thing. "You mean the magic is gone?" she said dramatically. "No chills or goose bumps?"

"Not even a rash." I smiled at her.

"You know something, Amy Miller? Writing this book is the best thing that ever happened to you."

I was about to agree when Lucy Skinner bounded over to the table like a frisky Labrador. "Bet you thought I forgot, didn't you?" She gave one of her booming laughs and plunked down a loaded tray that could have belonged to Henry the Eighth.

"Of course we didn't forget," Sharon said, always the perfect hostess. "Amy's been getting all this terrific material from Karen Clover, but there's plenty of room in the book for you."

"A whole chapter, maybe even two," I said seriously. Sharon gave me a sharp look, but I went right on talking. "As you said, Lucy, you've had your share of romances, and Sharon and I don't want to miss a single word. . . ." I took out my pen and gave her my most professional smile. "Now, where shall we start?"

She stared at me, thinking. I noticed she was wearing a shocking pink sweater, and plum lipstick, a terrible choice for someone with freckles. I didn't see how I could tell her though, so I wisely decided to keep quiet.

"I guess we'll have to go all the way back

to third grade," she said finally. "I had this mad crush on Gerald Payne who sat right in front of me in Miss Algers' class — "

"Well, that certainly sounds fascinating," I said, pushing back my chair and getting up. Out of the corner of my eye, I saw Lucy and Sharon staring at me, open-mouthed. I was reaching for my purse when Lucy finally found her tongue.

"You're leaving?" Lucy demanded in astonishment.

I put on a look of mock surprise. "Oh, didn't Sharon tell you that she's my collaborator? We've divided up the work," I said cheerily. I slung my book bag over my shoulder and picked up my tray. I could dump it, and still have time to buy a hot dog at the snack shop.

"What do you mean we've divided up the work?" Sharon said, smiling for Lucy's benefit.

"It's all part of the new system," I said innocently. "Don't you remember?" She opened her mouth to say something, but I beat her to it. "From now on we take turns doing the interviews." I passed her my notebook and pen, trying for a look of keen disappointment.

"Of course I'd love to stick around and listen in, but I have to do some research in the library. You know how it is with us writers — just work, work, work!"

"Now just a minute," Lucy objected. Her

pale face was flushed and her freckles stood out in sharp relief.

I leaned down and jabbed her in the shoulder. "Don't worry, she'll do a great job," I said with my mouth close to her ear. "Sharon's a great interviewer. Really the best. She has a way of making romance come alive."

I gave her another jab in the shoulder for good measure, and made a quick getaway.

"That was a dirty trick you played," Sharon said later that night. "Lucy rambled on so long, I was late for math class, and Mr. Tyler socked me with an extra half page of quadratic equations. 'To remind me to be on time,' he said. Hah!"

I laughed, and shifted the phone to a more comfortable position. "I'm sorry about the equations, Sharon, but it really was your own fault, you know. You never should have told any of the kids about the book — at least not without asking me." I was stretched out on my waterbed, my chin cupped in one hand, making a vain stab at a history report.

"Did you get any good material from her?" I couldn't resist asking. "I thought the part about Gerald Payne had great possibilities."

"Very funny," she said and gave a grudging laugh. "Just be glad you missed the part about Charley DeWitt."

"Charley DeWitt? Isn't he the senior with red hair and freckles? He and Lucy could almost pass for clones."

"Right. According to Lucy, she's been madly in love with him for six weeks, and he's the boy who *almost* asked her to the Senior Prom."

"Almost?" I said skeptically.

"He just happened to have a date with Julie Richards, that fantastic blonde who's head of the cheerleading squad."

"But if it hadn't been for Julie Richards, Charley and Lucy would have been dancing freckle to freckle."

"You're right. But instead, Lucy stayed home and cried her eyes out."

"I hate to say it, but it's going to be hard to build a paragraph around that," I laughed.

"A paragraph! Lucy thinks Charles De-Witt is worth a whole chapter!" She stopped long enough to take a bite out of an apple. "Isn't it funny how most people have absolutely no idea at all of what makes an interesting novel?"

"It's very strange," I agreed, wondering if she would catch the sarcasm.

She didn't. "Of course, not everyone has a flair for writing like we do," she conceded. "By the way," she went on, "have you gotten much down on paper yet?"

"Not a word," I said, wondering how I would ever finish my history paper by Monday.

"Amy!" she squealed. "I thought you'd have tons of stuff by now."

"Well, at least I've got a main character," I reminded her.

"That's true," she said, mollified. "Good old Simon. I really think he's kind of cute, don't you?"

"Of course," I snapped, beginning to feel a little annoyed. "I would never have picked him for the hero if I didn't," I reminded her.

"It's funny you never had a mad crush on him, isn't it," she said thoughtfully. "I mean, it's a good thing you didn't, because it would certainly complicate things."

"It would ruin everything," I agreed. "It's much better this way. I can just think of Simon as . . . material, and not involved." When I said that, a picture of a smiling Simon drifted across my mind — smiling, intelligent, friendly — and I felt that same guilty pang I had felt earlier. This is no time to get a prickly conscience, I told myself sternly. I need a romantic hero, and Simon is going to be it!

We talked for a few more minutes, and then I hung up to get back to my paper on the Roman Empire. I just couldn't get interested in viaducts and plumbing systems, though, and when the phone rang a few minutes later, I grabbed it on the first ring.

"You must have been sitting on the phone," a deep English voice said.

I laughed happily. Simon certainly didn't waste any time. And his voice on the phone was warm and exciting. I'd have to remember to make a note of that, I thought, reaching for my pad.

"I'm studying in bed," I told him, "and

the phone's right on the night table."

"Ah, I see," he said, and then there was dead silence.

I didn't mind though, because I was writing furiously. *His voice raced across the wires like* . . . I was momentarily stumped. *Warm molasses?* No, that was ridiculous. Molasses sounded Southern, and Simon was British. *Molten honey?* I was sure I had read that in one of Sharon's romance books. Or was it *molten gold?* I sighed and put a question mark next to *voice.* I'd have to figure it out later.

"I just wondered if everything was still on for tomorrow," he said. For the first time, I noticed a touch of shyness in his voice. Did he really think that maybe I didn't want to go out with him?

"Of course it is," I assured him. It had to be, I thought grimly. Simon didn't know it, but I was planning a whole first chapter around our day together.

"Well, I just wanted to remind you to wear some good running shoes. Some of the terrain I cover is pretty rocky, and it's easy to get shin splints. But on the whole, I really prefer to run on hills, don't you?"

I pretended to consider the problem. "On the whole, yes," I said finally. Run on hills? That brief sprint across the quad had nearly killed me.

"Just wanted to warn you," he said cheerily. "After all, five miles can be tough going in the wrong shoes."

Five miles! I felt the bottom drop out of my stomach. I'd *never* make five miles.

He hung up then, and I sat stunned. No one had told me that writing would be hazardous to my health!

Around ten, I wandered into the kitchen to get a quick snack, before falling into bed.

"How's the author?" Mom said, looking up from the popcorn maker "Dad and I are watching a great movie on TV." She looked at me expectantly. "*Anna Karenina*. Would you like to join us?"

"No thanks. I already know the plot," I sighed. I watched her sprinkle Parmesan cheese all over the popcorn. It seems like a really gross way to ruin a bowl of popcorn, but that's the way Dad likes it.

"Well, speaking of plots, how's your book going?"

I wondered if I should tell her about Simon. "It hasn't gotten off the ground yet, but I hope to work on it a lot this weekend." That was certainly a safe thing to say.

"I thought you had a date this weekend," she said, puzzled. "An all-day date, wasn't it? This new friend of yours must really be crazy about you."

I poured a glass of milk and sat down on the kitchen table. "No, he's just very athletic." I thought of the early morning run on Saturday and winced. Saturday was my one day to sleep in, and it would be a real drag to tumble out of bed at seven. This must be what Mrs. Harding meant when she talked about writers making sacrifices for their art!

"You haven't said much about him," Mom said, watching me carefully. "In fact, the only thing I know about him is that he's English."

"Oh, he's really nice," I said, trying to downplay the whole thing. "Let me see, he's got sandy hair and really nice eyes, and he uses a lot of English expressions — " I laughed remembering how Simon said the word *controversy*. He put the accent on the second syllable, which never failed to crack me up.

"He sounds cute. I can hardly wait to meet him," she said. The commercial was over then, and Dad called Mom back to the den to watch the rest of the movie. I would have liked to talk about Simon some more, but I knew Mom and Dad never have much time to spend together, so I decided to head back to my room. I was dead-tired, and expected to fall asleep immediately.

When I got back to my room, I realized that I had left the shutters open, and a balmy breeze was ruffling the papers on my desk. Worse, it was one of those achingly beautiful nights, when the sky is peppered with stars, and the moon hangs high like a pale silver globe. I've always been a sucker for moonlight, and after slipping into a light cotton nightgown, I curled up on my window seat, staring at the sky.

Just the kind of things romantic heroines do, I caught myself thinking, and laughed out loud. I wondered if I should make some notes for the book, and decided against it. There would be plenty of opportunity on Saturday.

Then it hit me; how could I possibly bring a notebook along when I went out with Simon? He'd think I was crazy, and naturally he'd be suspicious. There wouldn't be any logical way to explain it, unless . . . I noticed a battered old notebook sticking out from under my closet door. My freshman leaf collection. Surely the most boring project my biology teacher had invented. I'd spent weeks tramping through the woods, writing down the Latin names of dozens of varieties of leaves and wild flowers.

That would be the perfect cover! I'd simply tell Simon I was doing a biology project, and had to make notes on the trees and plants in Ridley Park. That would take care of part of the day, and as for the Italian restaurant — my powers of invention deserted me, and I crawled into bed. I'd have to play that scene by ear.

N*ine*

"He's here!" my mother hissed frantically. I opened one eye cautiously, and just as I suspected, bright sunlight slashed across it like a razor blade. I winced and burrowed back under the covers.

"Can't be," I muttered sleepily. "Much too early."

"It's not too early. It's six-thirty, and Simon Adams is here!"

Another cautious peek at the clock and I knew she was right. I was debating what to do next when my mother solved the problem for me; she yanked all the covers off the bed.

"C'mon, the least you can do is get up," she said irritably. She clutched her pink terry bathrobe tightly around her, and ran a hand through her hair. "You think you've got problems — all you've got to do is tumble out of bed. I had to go answer the door looking like this!"

I groaned and started to get up.

"You get a move on in here and I'll throw some clothes on and see if he'd like some coffee while he's waiting."

"Thanks, Mom," I said.

She paused at the doorway. "Oh, and Amy," she said smiling.

"Yes?"

"He seems nice."

"He is," I said.

I sighed and picked up my leaf identification book. That plus my notebook and pen were all the tools I needed. I dressed quickly and stared at myself in the mirror. In my white short-sleeved blouse and tan camp shorts, I didn't look like a romance writer at all. I could easily pass for Amy Miller, girl botanist.

When I bounced down the stairs a few minutes later, two things hit me at once: the smell of frying bacon, and Simon's English accent. He must have been telling a hilariously funny story, because I could hear Mom and Matthew laughing their heads off.

He had just delivered the punch line when I gingerly pushed open the swinging door to the kitchen. The three of them were sitting at the round oak table, nearly doubled over, giggling and wiping their eyes.

As soon as he spotted me, Simon beamed and jumped up. "Hi, Amy. Your mother tells me I got you out of bed. Sorry about that — sometimes I forget that not everyone is a morning person."

Why had she told him that! I shot a look at my mother.

"Oh, that's okay," I said cheerfully. "I'm always up six or six-thirty at the latest. I don't know why the alarm didn't go off this time."

"Maybe because you didn't set it," Matthew said.

I glared at him and nibbled at a piece of bacon. I noticed Simon was sipping orange juice and raised my eyebrows.

"I offered him breakfast," my mother said, catching my look, "but he said he had already eaten at home."

"That's right," Simon said, patting his flat stomach. "Besides, it's better not to load up too much before running. It interferes with the blood supply to the muscles," he said seriously. "Lactic acid buildup, and all that."

"Oh, absolutely," I agreed. I wolfed down the last of the bacon and reached for a blueberry muffin. "That's why I hardly touch a bite on days I run," I added casually.

"Days you run?" Matthew said, puzzled. I wanted to kick him, swiftly, under the table, but he was sitting too far away.

"Tell me, Simon," my mother said breezily, "how do you like living in America?" I don't know if she really was curious, or if she was trying to rescue me from Matthew's annoying questions.

"Oh, it's great," Simon said politely. "Everyone's been so friendly to my family and me. I've gotten to do a lot of new things, and I've met some special people, like Amy," he said, turning to smile at me.

I smiled back, feeling like a female Benedict Arnold. He wouldn't think I was so special if he knew what I was planning.

"I've always thought it would be nice to visit England on my own," my mother was saying wistfully. "The last time I was there, I had to shepherd thirty-five grade school kids around." She shuddered at the memory. "I remember when little Sheila Thomas got lost in the Tower of London. . . ."

I knew there was no stopping Mom when she got started on one of her travel stories, so I leaned back and relaxed, sneaking another muffin at the same time. It was the perfect opportunity to study Simon. He was sitting right next to me and I looked him over very cooly and objectively, just as a writer should.

I decided to be logical about it and start at the top. Hair: thick and sandy-colored, worn a little long over the ears. Profile: perfect. If ever there was a ten, this was it. It's funny, I thought with a funny little quiver inside, I've never realized before just how good-looking Simon really is. He has what the books call "finely chiseled features," with a straight nose, high cheekbones, and a great chin. And flashing dark eyes and a movie-star smile.

Sharon's words floated back to me: He's cute, isn't he? Yes, I thought, Simon Adams is definitely cute. Well, so much the better, I decided, wishing I could reach for my notebook.

A burst of laughter jolted me, and I realized that Mom was winding up her Sheila Thomas story. If I didn't move fast, she'd be bound to start in on the one about the two schoolteachers who had missed the boat. train and were stranded overnight in Calais.

"Uh, we really should be going, Mom," I said, jumping up. I took a swig of orange juice and grabbed my notebook.

"Oh, I didn't mean to keep you two from your run," she said.

"That's quite all right, Mrs. Miller," Simon said gallantly. "You've had some really great experiences. Maybe you can tell us about them later today. . . ."

That was carrying politeness a little too far, I thought, but I smiled brightly. "Well, are you all set, Simon? I can hardly wait to hit the trail." Hit the trail! I had already picked up runner's lingo.

I saw Matthew squirming, out of the corner of my eye, but I grabbed Simon's arm and nudged him toward the door. I rushed him through his good-byes, and we finally found ourselves on the front porch. In just a few minutes, we'd be "on the trail," wherever that was.

But to my surprise, Simon made no move to leave the front porch. "Do you want to do a few lunges before we get started?" he asked.

Lunges? "Sure," I said confidently. I had no idea what he was talking about.

Simon immediately spread his legs like a scissors and moved gracefully from side to side, just inches off the floor. "I got a pretty bad sprain the last time I forgot to warm up," he said casually, "so I try to do fifty of these every time now."

"Good idea," I said wisely. *Fifty!* I squatted clumsily on the porch and tried to imitate Simon. It was impossible, of course, because he was like one of the stick insects with a hundred joints that can bend in any direction. I made a few tentative lurches to the left and right, and immediately got a cramp. Luckily, Simon was too busy with his fifty lunges to notice the trouble I was having, and finally he took a deep breath and stood up.

"That feels much better," he said, rubbing his calf thoughtfully. He smiled at me, and turned up the collar on his navy windbreaker. "All set?"

I forced a grin and picked up my gear — notebook, leaf guide and pen. "As ready as I'll ever be," I told him. That was certainly the truth.

"Then let's hit the road!"

Half an hour later, I knew I was a candidate for a coronary care ward. Simon and I had begun by jogging eight blocks to a state park. The jogging wasn't too bad, because I got a chance to catch my breath at traffic lights and crossings. A couple of times I even pretended to drop my notebook, which gave me a few precious seconds to fall to my knees and scoop it up.

The park was a different story completely. As soon as we got to the edge of the "wilderness trail," Simon turned to me excitedly.

"What do you think, Amy? There's three paths: beginner, experienced, and expert. Shall we go for the toughest one?"

"Why not?" I said recklessly.

"That's my girl," he answered cheerfully. Suddenly he turned and darted up a hillside, as confidently as a mountain goat. Stunned, I scrambled to follow him, my leg muscles already rebelling against the steep uphill climb.

"The trail goes straight up for half a mile or so," he tossed over his shoulder, "and then it tapers off into a nice clearing before it continues."

"Good," I gasped. A nice clearing was just what I needed, I thought, as I stubbed my toe on a boulder. I longed for a place where I could flop down on the grass, stare at the sky, and let my pulse return to normal. I was glad that Simon was in front, so he couldn't see me wheezing and stumbling along the rocky path. He was running easily, his blue windbreaker unzipped to catch the morning breeze, as happy as a gerbil on an exercise wheel.

"Nice day for running," he yelled back after a few minutes.

Did he really expect us to talk and run at the same time? I took in a big breath and managed to sputter, "It sure is. We'll have to do this again."

He turned and flashed a quick grin. "That's fine with me."

He thought I was serious! Once I got enough material for chapter one, I had no intention of ever setting foot on a wilderness trail again.

I was daydreaming about locations for chapters two and three — maybe a movie, or a restaurant, but definitely someplace where I could sit down — when Simon suddenly dropped back and began running alongside me.

"How are you doing?" he said, his voice concerned.

I waited a few seconds before I answered, hoping my voice wouldn't show how out of breath I was. "Great!" I said, forcing an enthusiasm I didn't feel. Actually, I felt like my chest was going to explode any minute. Why had I been crazy enough to tell Simon I was a runner?

"You seem a little winded," he said politely.

"Winded?" I managed a fake laugh, and brushed a clump of hair out of my eyes. "Oh no, I could do this all day. How about you?" I said, hoping to get him talking about himself.

"Oh, this is an easy run for me," he said lightly. "I try to do six miles a day, sometimes eight on the weekends, unless I have a lot of homework."

I nodded, knowing I didn't have the strength for another penetrating question. "Hmmm," I managed to say thoughtfully.

Luckily, Simon didn't need much encouragement to talk about running. For the next few minutes, he told me all about the different tracks he had run on, the best types of shoes to avoid shin splints, and the importance of keeping a running schedule.

"I guess it's a good thing I'm a compulsive person," he said laughingly, "or I'd never have the discipline to get out here every morning at five-thirty. Someone told me once I must have an obsessive personality."

"You, too?" I blurted out, forgetting I was supposed to save my breath for running. "It's funny, someone told me the same thing a couple of weeks ago."

Simon's eyes lit up with interest. "That is a coincidence. What's your obsession, Amy?"

My obsession! Why did I have such a big mouth? I could hardly tell him I had an obsession about boys, and I struggled to come up with something that sounded believable.

"I have an obsession about — " My eyes darted frantically around for inspiration, and finally landed on my leaf identification book. "Leaves!" I said triumphantly. It sounded bizarre, I suppose, but anything was better than the truth.

Simon looked so puzzled, I burst out laughing, losing a lot of precious oxygen. If the trail kept on winding upward any higher, I'd probably black out before we ever reached the top. And how would I ever explain that to Simon?

"Not just leaves," I said, slowing down my pace a little, "but all kinds of plants and shrubs." In a burst of invention, I reached over and pulled a silvery leaf from a bush growing alongside the trail. I jogged a little slower, so I could show it to Simon.

He looked at it and shrugged. "What's special about it?" he asked.

"What's special?" I said in a shocked tone. "You mean you don't recognize a *phillus robilligosis* when you see one?" I shook my head sadly, and tucked the leaf into a zipper pocket on my jacket. "People can collect leaves for years and not find one of these.".

"Honestly?" Simon was looking at me with a new respect. "You're really into this, aren't you?"

"Of course I am," I said quietly. I gestured to bushes and trees around us. "We're surrounded by tons of exciting plants here. If it's okay with you, I'd like to stop and make a few notes when we reach the clearing."

"That's fine with me," Simon said quickly. "I see you came prepared." He pointed to my notebook.

"Yes, I always do," I told him seriously. "I just never know when I'll spot something, and have to make a note about it." I paused and smiled at him. "So I'll probably be scribbling away all day. That won't bother you, will it?"

"Bother me? Of course not." He reached over and touched my arm very lightly. "I like a girl who has a lot of interests."

He liked me! At first I felt elated, and then a wave of something else washed over me. I recognized it immediately.

Guilt.

Simon liked me and I felt like a first-class rat.

Ten

"How did it go?" Sharon squealed a few hours later. "I want to hear every juicy detail." Sharon's voice always sounds about three octaves higher on the phone, and I had to hold the receiver a few inches away from my ear.

"It's not over yet," I said wearily. I was leaning against the kitchen counter, trying to summon up the energy to shower and change before my pizza date with Simon. I gave her a quick rundown on the day. "We're going out to dinner in a couple of hours, and then we might go to a movie."

"Great!" she said. "I know you'll get tons of fantastic material tonight. "It's supposed to be a full moon," she said coyly. "Just don't get so carried away you forget to take notes," she teased.

"No chance of that," I said shortly. "Writers are supposed to be objective, remember?"

"I know that. I was only kidding," she apologized. "Well, have you learned anything interesting so far?"

"I've discovered I don't like tofu."

"What?"

"Tofu," I explained, "is supposed to be a vegetarian treat. It's some kind of white bean curd, cut in little squiggly squares — "

"Yuck," she said feelingly. "What does tofu have to do with you?"

"Unfortunately, quite a bit," I said wryly. "It turns out that Simon is a strict vegetarian, and he made us tofu sandwiches for lunch."

"Oh." She paused, thinking. " I don't think that's anything we want to include in the book," she said finally.

"Why not?"

She laughed. "Well, somehow I just can't picture a romantic scene over tofu, if it's as bad as you say it is."

"Maybe it's an acquired taste," I said, wondering why I was springing to Simon's defense. I was sorry I had told Sharon about the tofu. Somehow it seemed like a betrayal of Simon, even though I hadn't intended it that way.

"You sound kind of beat," Sharon said sympathetically.

"I am." I yawned, wondering how I was going to get through the evening. The hike and bike ride had taken more out of me than I realized, and I still had to manage dinner and the movie. "Look, Sharon, I think I better hang up so I can organize my notes while they're still fresh in my mind."

"Go ahead," she said encouragingly. "Let's get together tomorrow afternoon and start on the first draft, okay? The book's going to be dynamite, I just know it!"

"Sure," I said, trying for a note of enthusiasm. I was so tired, I didn't even know if I would be alive tomorrow afternoon!

I stood under the shower a long time, letting the blasting hot water sting my aching legs, and thought about Simon. For some reason, I can always think better, when I'm soaking wet, surrounded by a cloud of steam. Sharon swears there's some deep psychological reason for that, but I'm not sure I agree with her.

I closed my eyes and let my mind wander over the events of the day, ticking off the high points and the low ones. After a few minutes, I realized something interesting. With the exception of the tofu, the day had been all high points! Simon had been the ideal "date" in every way, and would make the perfect romantic hero for my book. My instincts had been right, after all.

I couldn't have dreamed up a better character, even if I had wanted to. Simon was one of the most exciting boys I had ever met. He was interesting, had a great sense of humor, and made me feel like I was someone special. I was thinking about the best way to capture him on paper, when Matthew pounded on the door.

"Amy, will you get a move on?" he yelled. "I've got to get in there to wash my hair."

"Okay, okay," I said, huffily. Matthew is the only boy I know who spends more time on his hair than I do. Whenever he goes on a date, he pulls out all the stops, using a special shampoo and a conditioning treatment that comes in a fake rawhide bottle.

I turned off the water, and wrapped myself in a giant terry towel. I took a quick look in the mirror and noticed my face was bright pink, like I had just stepped out of a sauna.

Later in my room, I debated what to wear. Something frilly and feminine? Or should I aim for a slightly punk look with oversized earrings and a new denim miniskirt?

What would Simon like? I caught myself thinking, and then had to smile. I was the one plotting the evening, not him!

I threw open my closet doors and tried to picture what a "romantic heroine" would choose. Nothing seemed quite right until I spied a soft cotton skirt that one of Mom's clients had brought back from Mexico. It reminds me of a sunset, because the colors change from orange to tangerine to gold. It's very soft and gauzy and has black embroidery around the waist. I tried it on — it was perfect.

I brushed my hair upside down for five minutes to give it body, and decided to wear it loose, hanging to my shoulders. Then I added tiny gold heart-shaped earrings and a thin gold chain.

Finally, I sat down at my desk, and flipped open my notebook. Some of the scrawls I had made that day were almost unintelligible, but a few stood out. They all were about Simon, naturally. It was hard to believe that they would form the basis for a first chapter.

A funny way of raising one eyebrow when he's surprised.

His lips curve in a smile as if he's just heard something wonderful.

His eyes are dark, but have flecks of gold in them.

He laughs easily.

When he talks, he leans forward, and makes you feel like you're the most fascinating person in the world.

I heard the doorbell ring, and jumped up to make a final check in the mirror. Not bad, I decided, watching the Mexican skirt swirl around my legs. It had a handkerchief hem, and made my legs look very long.

Simon didn't stand a chance.

"You take your botany seriously," Simon said wryly. We were sitting in a back booth at Luigi's, my favorite Italian restaurant, and I was trying to decide between stuffed shells and tortellini.

"My botany?" I said absently. I smiled, and leaned back into the soft red leather cushion. All the fresh air and exercise had made me feel a little drowsy, and my mind was churning in slow motion.

He smiled and pointed to my notebook. "Are you going to take notes about the hanging baskets? I hate to tell you, but I think they're filled with rubber plants."

"Oh that!" I stammered, and closed my hand protectively over the notebook. I could have kicked myself for leaving it out on the table — what if he had opened it? The whole game would be up!

"I've never seen such dedication," he went on smoothly, giving me a very intense look that made me feel funny inside.

"Actually," I gulped, "this is for my mother.

"Your mother?" The eyebrow shot up again. It was his left one, I noticed, and I had an insane urge to grab the book and make a note about it.

"Yes, she's very interested in pasta." I smiled tolerantly, as if there was no accounting for taste. "In fact, she's taking an Italian cooking course, and she asked me to jot down the names of some dishes for her."

"I'm sure they'd let you take a menu home," Simon said helpfully. "We could ask the waiter when he comes back."

"That's a great idea," I gushed, "but of course, I want to make a few notes myself. You can tell me what your vegetarian spaghetti is like," I said, hoping to throw him off guard. Simon had already announced that he was going to order spaghetti with peas and mushrooms in it.

"It's called pasta primavera," he said, just as the waiter came back to take our orders. I hurriedly chose the tortellini, and after the waiter had left, Simon and I smiled at each other across the table.

"Athletes eat a lot of carbohydrates, don't they?" I said. I had no idea if they really did, but I had seen a newspaper headline about it that morning.

"There's two schools of thought on that," Simon said very seriously. "Some coaches think that it's good to force carbohydrates a couple of hours before an event. . . ."

I knew that once I got Simon talking about exercise, I could relax and study him. I gave him my "bright-interested" look, and he rambled on happily. I really didn't care if people could run faster on spaghetti or candy bars, but I was glad that Simon had found something he liked to talk about.

As casually as I could, I slid my notebook in front of me, and began idly scrawling a quick description of Luigi's. All I needed were a few words that would help me reconstruct the scene later, I decided. Red-checkered tablecloths, wine bottles with wax dripping down the sides, soft music drifting in from another room. . . .

"What are you doing?" Simon stopped talking suddenly and was frowning.

"You don't mind if I write this down, do

you?" I said innocently. "I've got to write a paper for health class sometime next month, and I was thinking of doing it on sports and nutrition."

"No, I don't mind at all," he said, brightening. "I'm no expert," he added with a shrug. "These are just tips that I've picked up during the past year."

"Is that when you first got interested in running?" I said in my best interview voice. Anything to keep him talking!

"We had a hiking club in England," he began. "We didn't do anything that strenuous, but there are some wonderful hills in the north part of the country. But I guess you know that," he said apologetically.

"No, I don't know much about England," I said, hoping to encourage him. "Especially the area that you're from. Yorkshire, isn't it?"

"That's right," he said eagerly. "You should see it in the summer, Amy. Heather grows wild on the moors, and it's so thick it covers everything like a blanket. And there's a little place called Staithes that has cliffs that drop straight down to the sea. . . ."

I nodded and smiled, tucking away bits of information for the book. Simon didn't know it, but he was writing the first chapter for me!

It wasn't until much later, when we were digging into our ice cream, that the talk turned more personal.

"I like your hearts," he said casually. "Is there some significance to them?"

"My hearts?" I asked blankly.

He reached over and lightly touched my ears. "These," he said, letting his hand linger a little longer than was absolutely necessary.

"Oh, they were a birthday present last year," I said, flushing a little. "No, there's no special significance to them. Why do you ask?"

"Just wondering. I thought maybe they were from an admirer."

He meant a boy, of course, so I decided to set the record straight.

"Sharon Blakely gave them to me," I explained. "She's my best friend. I was born in March." He hadn't even asked when my birthday was. So why was I telling him?

"You're a Pisces," he said thoughtfully. "That sheds a lot of light on things, you know."

"It does?"

"Definitely." To my amazement, he reached across the table and took my hand. "That explains why you're so warm, and funny, and interested in people."

"You can tell all that?" I said a little nervously. I wasn't sure I liked it when Simon started to analyze me. In another minute, he'd be telling me I had thin boundaries.

"Pisces are very involved with their feelings," he said seriously. "They tend to form very strong attachments, but you've probably already discovered that for yourself."

He smiled at me, and I felt a little uneasy. Had he heard about my twenty-three crushes? No, it was impossible. Even Sharon would never break a confidence like that!

"I guess I am a little emotional," I said lightly. "I cry at movies, and at good-byes."

"You do? I'll have to remember that," he said, giving my hand a little squeeze and finally releasing it. His ice cream had melted on his dish in a rainbow of colors, and I was dying to make a note of it, but Simon didn't give me a chance. Before I could pick up the pen, he was standing up and reaching for the check.

"If we're going to make that movie, we better get started," he said.

"You're on," I told him.

Half an hour later, we were settled with popcorn and Cokes in the darkened Park Theatre, and I tried to focus my attention on the screen. It was a Woody Allen movie that I had already seen, and I caught myself sneaking sideways glances at Simon. His profile was wonderful I noticed again; when he tilted his head back to laugh, I found myself smiling, too.

Finally we finished the popcorn and drinks and Simon casually rested his arm on the back of my seat. *Interesting*, I decided, as the arm dropped to my shoulders and stayed there. Simon kept staring at the screen, as if he had a robot arm with a mind of its own.

I giggled at the image — and wondered if I could use it in the book — when he turned and looked at me.

"Enjoying the movie?" he said in his low voice.

"Very much. Woody Allen is one of my favorites."

"We have a lot in common." He gave my arm a little squeeze. "We'll have to do this more often," he said softly. "I think they're having a Woody Allen festival next week. . . ." His voice trailed off and he looked at me questioningly. "Unless you have other plans?"

Hah! Simon *was* my plan, and he didn't even know it. "No other plans," I told him.

"That's good." He sighed happily. "Because I want to spend a lot of time with you, Amy."

A minute later, he reached over and took my hand in his. "I'm so glad I met you," he murmured.

"Me, too," I whispered. I forced myself to look back at the screen then, fighting down a quiver of excitement. Simon was playing into my hands perfectly. Movies, pizza dates, jogging, picnics . . . and an English hero.

What a dynamite book this would make!

$E^{\underline{leven}}$

"This is all you've got?" Sharon said incredulously. She flipped all the way through my notebook and then turned back to the front. "Just two pages?"

"It's not easy taking notes on a date," I told her. "After all, I couldn't make Simon suspicious, could I? That would blow the whole thing sky-high."

"I suppose you're right," she sighed. "Still, it doesn't leave us much to work with." She poured herself a cup of orange delight tea. Even though it was early Sunday morning, Sharon looked sensational, as usual, in a khaki jumpsuit with tan leather trim. Her blonde hair was gleaming and she had swept it back off her face with two tortoiseshell barrettes. I had gone for a more casual look with bare feet, a battered pair of navy-blue gym shorts, and a Mickey Mouse T-shirt.

"We've got plenty of material here," I insisted. "It's what we do with it that's important."

I was speaking in a low voice, even though I didn't think our voices would carry upstairs. The house was eerily quiet, since my parents and Matthew were still sleeping.

Sharon and I had decided to work on the kitchen table, after she had taken one look at my room and pronounced it a disaster area. "Don't you know that a cluttered room is a sign of a cluttered mind?" she'd muttered. She'd picked up her tea and sweet rolls and marched straight back into the kitchen.

"Take another look at my notes," I urged her. "There's certainly enough there for a first chapter."

"I suppose you're right," she admitted grudgingly. "I like the descriptions. Do Simon's eyes really have flecks of gold in them?"

"When the light hits them a certain way," I said.

Sharon looked up from scanning my notes and said teasingly, "Something tells me you left out the best part of the evening. Or maybe it's not for publication?"

"The best part?"

"You know what I'm talking about," she insisted. "I don't see a word in here about kissing."

"Kissing," I stammered. "I didn't mention

kissing because . . . there wasn't any." I suddenly felt a little uncomfortable, and jumped up to make another pot of tea.

Sharon was giving me a funny sideways glance with her enormous blue eyes, and I felt compelled to explain. "We shook hands at the end of the evening," I said, standing at the stove, pretending to be busy fiddling around with the kettle.

"You shook hands! Is that the way they say good-night in England?" Sharon said archly.

"I . . . uh . . . don't think so."

"Well, honestly Amy, don't keep me in suspense! What happened? Why didn't he kiss you?"

"I think he was going to, but we were kind of interrupted. The whole evening had gone so perfectly, and then suddenly we were standing close together on my front porch. I told Simon I had a wonderful time and thanked him — "

"And what did he say?" she interrupted.

"Oh, the usual. He said that he'd had a great time, too, and that he'd like to see me again."

"And. . . ." Sharon was leaning forward, her eyes bright and interested.

"And then we heard a car door slam, and Matthew came tearing up the stairs." I laughed. "It shattered the moment completely."

"But he *would* have kissed you," Sharon insisted.

"I'd like to think so — strictly from a literary point of view."

Sharon sighed. "Well, make sure he does next time," she said darkly. "We can't base a whole chapter on holding hands," she said, glancing at the notes I'd made during the movie.

"I'll do my best," I said dryly. "Anyway, I'm going to have lots more dates with him. He's already asked me out to the Woody Allen festival, and to that new disco on South Street, and we're going jogging again — "

"Hold on," Sharon said, laughing. "It sounds like you're going to have enough material for ten books if you keep on at that rate."

"Hey, that's an idea. I could write a trilogy. Or maybe even a series."

A couple of hours later, Matthew staggered in for breakfast, and Sharon and I beat a hasty retreat to my bedroom. By this time, we had chosen a name for the hero — Sean Anderson — and were hard at work on the first chapter when the phone rang.

I reached over and picked it up, my eyes riveted to my notebook.

"Hello," I said absently, wondering if Sean Anderson should have a "low, husky voice," or a "husky, low voice." It's funny how you never notice things like that in books, until you struggle to write one yourself.

"Hello, Amy," a voice said. A voice that was definitely "low, husky," I caught myself

111

thinking and then nearly fell off the bed in surprise. It was Simon.

"Uh, hi," I repeated inanely, wishing Sharon weren't listening to every word. "I hadn't expected to hear from you so soon," I added, in what had to be one of the dumbest remarks ever made.

"Tired of me already?" he said lightly.

"No, of course not," I said, feeling Sharon's eyes on me. I scrunched up with my knees to my chest, wondering what I could do to save the conversation. I idly thought of asking Sharon to go make us another pot of tea, but she sat solidly on my desk chair, watching me like a hawk.

"I had a good time yesterday," I said finally. I looked over at Sharon, like an actor in the middle of an audition. She nodded approvingly.

"I'm glad. I was afraid we might have overdone the jogging a little. If you're sore, you can always take a hot bath, you know. That really eases the muscles."

"I'll remember that," I said, and then there was dead silence. For some reason, my tongue was permanently stalled, and nothing would get it in motion again. Or maybe it was my brain that was stalled. I couldn't think of a single thing to say!

Sharon could, though. She jabbed me in the arm, and handed me a piece of paper. "Make sure he asks you out!"

I was wondering how I was supposed to do that, when Simon said hesitantly, "This is kind of last minute, and I suppose you've got plans, but I was wondering if you were free today. . . ."

"Oh yes, I'm free. I'm not doing anything important at all," I said recklessly. Brilliant! Now he'd think I was one of those girls who hang around the house waiting for a boy to call. "What did you have in mind?" I added.

"Well, there's an art exhibit in Harper Park today, and there's also an international food festival. I thought maybe we could go to both. If I picked you up at twelve, we could look at the paintings for a while, and then have lunch at the festival."

"That sounds wonderful," I said, looking in dismay at my wrinkled shorts. I'd have to rush like a maniac to pull myself together.

"Good, I was hoping you'd say that." He sounded relieved. "I knew you weren't one of those girls who takes hours to get ready."

"Oh, no, not at all," I said, already reaching for my hairbrush. "I like to be spontaneous."

"So do I," Simon said. "See you in half an hour."

I had barely replaced the receiver when Sharon squealed happily.

"Did he ask you out for next Saturday?"

"He asked me out for — now!" I said, leaping off the bed. I raced to the closet and started pulling out clothes. What do you wear to an art exhibit? Or to a food festival? I turned to Sharon.

"Sharon, you've got to help me," I said

desperately. "If you were going to spend the whole day in Harper Park — "

"Why in the world would I want to do that?" she interrupted.

"To look at paintings and eat food," I said curtly.

"Oh, you mean the art exhibit, and the international food festival!" she said, understanding. "They had a big piece in the paper about that today."

"Sharon, please! Just tell me what you'd wear."

"That's easy," she said promptly. "I'd wear my new stone-washed jeans with my yellow oversized blouse, a wheat-colored macrame belt, and olive-green ankle boots. And then I'd tie a tomato-red cardigan sweater around my shoulders and let the sleeves dangle in the front. . . . I'd keep the jewelry simple. Just an Inca silver bracelet and tiny silver hoop earrings. My purse would be macrame, to match the belt, naturally."

I knew I shouldn't have asked Sharon.

I dove into my closet, ignoring her questions, and came up with a not-too-wrinkled pair of jeans, and a pale blue knit top. I knew I'd never find *my* ankle boots, so I decided to go with my sneakers. They were a little grundgy, but the grass might be damp in the park, anyway.

"I don't understand," Sharon was saying irritably. "How come you're going to the park now, with Simon?"

"Because he asked me," I said, my voice muffled. I was deep inside my closet, sorting through my scarf box. I finally found a red bandanna and held it up triumphantly. "I knew it was here someplace," I said happily. It would make a nice touch with the blue top, and I knotted it around my neck.

"But this is crazy!" Sharon said. "You don't need to go out with him today — you should wait until next Saturday!"

I stopped and looked at her. "What are you talking about? I thought you wanted me to go out with him. You said we need more material."

"Well, yes of course," she admitted, "but we already have more than enough for the first chapter. The whole problem, Amy, is that you're not organized about this."

She flipped open her yellow legal pad, and looked at me sternly. "You know we agreed to set certain goals for each day. Today, we introduced the boy — "

"Sean Anderson," I said automatically.

"And we made a pretty good start on the plot. . . ."

I nodded. The plot revolved around a classic situation — a love triangle. The heroine, Melissa Crane, was hopelessly in love with handsome Sean Anderson, but couldn't do anything about it, because her best friend — Trudy Phillips — was also in love with him! In fact, Sean and Trudy were going steady, and unless something drastic happened, it would be one of those stories of "unrequited love" that Mrs. Harding had talked about.

"Anyway, I guess I don't see what you're getting at," I said, throwing a brush and lipstick in my purse.

"The point, I'm *getting at*," Sharon said icily, "is that we're not going to get a book done, if you run off every time the phone rings. We had agreed to finish chapter one today." She picked up her notebook and stared at me, frowning.

"Sharon, our schedule wasn't written in stone," I said, getting a little annoyed myself. "You mean I'm only supposed to go out with Simon when we run out of material?"

"That's it, exactly."

I groaned and shook my head in disbelief. There are times when Sharon simply isn't reasonable, and this was one of them.

"Look," I said, fastening a gold chain around my neck, "we can't turn down a chance like this. Okay, so we've got more than we need for chapter one. . . ."

"We sure do," she insisted. "The tofu scene could take up two or three pages, and the Italian restaurant could be at least half a chapter. Plus the jogging scene," she reminded me.

"But don't you see?" I smiled at her. "We'll get some terrific stuff today: an art exhibit and a food festival. There are lots of romantic possibilities there."

"Well, make sure you take advantage of

116

them," she said, finally. She was still miffed, but I could see that she was weakening a little. "And make sure you do more than hold hands," she said pointedly.

"I'll do my very best." I held up two fingers in a Boy Scout salute, and Sharon cracked up. "Now do I have your permission to go on my date . . . er, I mean, my research assignment?"

"Of course," she said, smiling. "But remember, Amy, think *kissing*. Lots of kissing!"

Twelve

"You look great today," Simon said softly.

"I do?" I blurted out. I've never been great at handling compliments, and for some reason, I felt a little shy with Simon.

"Take my word for it, you do," he laughed. "I love that blue top," he said appreciatively.

He was holding my hand as we wandered through the rows of stalls at Harper Park, stopping occasionally to look at a painting or a piece of pottery. Simon and I discovered that we liked exactly the same things. We both loved abstract art — the wilder the better — and we admired the smooth stone pottery that was on display.

"I like things done in earth colors, don't you?" Simon said, picking up a small terra cotta fish. "I bet this is what your American desert looks like," he said, running his hand lightly over the sand-colored figure. "Look how the colors run together. The artist blended them perfectly. . . ."

"Like a sunset," I agreed.

He smiled, pleased. "I'm going to buy it for you," he said impulsively.

"Oh, Simon, no."

But I was too late. He was already handing some cash to a young woman behind the booth, and I watched as she carefully wrapped the fish in a cotton-lined box.

"Simon, you shouldn't have done that," I protested as he placed the box in my hands.

"Why not?" he said, surprised. "It's my first present to you," he said solemnly. "And you were born under the sign of the fish, weren't you?" He smiled at me.

"Yes, but . . . I don't know how to thank you," I stammered.

"Just promise to think of all the fun we had today — every time you look at it." He gave my hand a little squeeze. "My favorite Pisces." He said it so softly I could barely hear him.

Simon put on his sunglasses then, and threw his arm lightly around my shoulders. I sneaked a look at his strong profile, and knew the moment would be etched in my mind forever. The cloudless sky, the warm wind that ruffled Simon's sandy hair, the twinkle of wind chimes somewhere far off in the distance. They were all part of a sunny kaleidoscope that would remain locked in my memory.

And locked on paper, I reminded myself. Because today, after all, was the beginning of chapter two.

"Seen enough of the art show?" he asked, and I pulled my attention back to him.

"If you're suggesting lunch," I told him, "you're on! I'm starving."

"I didn't realize how late it was," he said apologetically, as we set off for the food festival at the opposite end of the park. "I hope all the booths are still open. Sometimes the popular stuff sells out fast."

"I'm sure we'll find something interesting," I said encouragingly.

As it turned out, I was overly optimistic. Simon immediately spotted a vegetarian booth and ordered a pita-and-tofu sandwich, but I wandered listlessly up and down the aisles searching for pizza or a hot dog.

"Nothing turns you on?" Simon said, coming up behind me. "You can always share my tofu," he offered, grinning. I had already told him that tofu appealed to me about as much as a large, wet eraser. "I'll make a convert out of you yet," he promised.

I made a face at him, and finally chose a Korean rice and pork dish with an unpronounceable name. After Simon paid for it, we found a picnic table on a grassy knoll overlooking the river.

"This reminds me of a place I used to go to in England," he said, staring at the rushing water. "My hiking club always used to stop for lunch by a stream. . . ." His voice trailed off, and there was a wistful expression on his face.

"You miss it, don't you?" I asked softly. "Home, I mean."

He nodded. "Sometimes. I'm really glad my father's company transferred him to the States, though. I've always wanted to come here, ever since I was a little kid." He laughed and bit into his sandwich. "I remember my mother took me to a Western movie when I was six, and I thought that all Americans wore cowboy hats and carried six-shooters."

"We must be a big disappointment to you then," I teased him.

"Are you kidding?" He reached across the table then and clasped my hand in his. "I'm not disappointed, Amy. Meeting you has been the best thing that ever happened to me," he said fervently. "I'm so glad you came into my life."

A family with little kids asked if they could share our picnic table just then, and Simon pulled back his hand, embarrassed. In a way, I was glad that something had happened to break the intensity of the moment. There had been something so special in the way Simon had looked at me, that I wanted time to think, time to savor it, and yes, time to figure out how to use it in chapter two!

Later in the afternoon, Simon left me alone for a few minutes while he went to buy us lemonade. I was sitting on a smooth, flat rock by the river, watching the sunset, when

I realized it was the perfect opportunity to jot down a few notes. I checked to make sure Simon was out of sight, and then pulled out my notebook. I scribbled a few lines about the art exhibit and the restaurant festival, and then wondered how to describe my relationship with Simon. We were friends more than anything else, I suppose. We had fun together, we held hands, but he hadn't even kissed me! I smiled, remembering Sharon's admonition. "Think kissing," she'd said. At the rate I was going, I'd have to rely on my imagination. . . .

"Writing your memoirs?" Simon's voice cut into my thoughts like a knife, and I nearly fell off my perch.

"No, I'm just — just putting together an article for the school paper," I said hastily. I crammed the notebook back in my purse and scooted over so Simon could sit next to me.

"I didn't know you wrote for the paper," Simon said, frowning a little. "I've never seen your by-line."

"That's because I'm just starting," I said, improvising wildly. "Mrs. Harding suggested I give it a try, and I thought the festival would be a great topic."

"I'll have to be very careful what I say around you from now on," Simon said, lowering himself onto the rock.

"What do you mean?" I gave a nervous laugh.

"Well, everybody knows reporters can be

dangerous," he said, smiling. "I'd hate to walk into school on Monday morning, and find that everything I said was front-page news."

"Oh that won't happen," I said, forcing a merry note into my voice. "I just cover arts and entertainment, not . . . personalities. You won't be in the story at all."

"I'm glad to hear it. I kind of like having my privacy. Did I tell you that my family was interviewed dozens of times when we first came over here?"

"We saw an article in the city newspaper about you," I told him.

"Six different papers interviewed us," Simon said ruefully. "At first it was fun, but after I saw the way my words were twisted up in print, I vowed never to talk to a reporter again."

"They misquoted you?" I said, surprised.

"Probably not intentionally. The reporters were just busy and overworked. They didn't really have enough time to spend with me, so the whole thing was pretty superficial." He laughed, and sipped his lemonade. "I sounded like the world's biggest idiot," he confessed. "One paper said that I was very depressed to find that you couldn't get scones and crumpets in the States. Everybody back home roared at that one."

"Is that true?"

He smiled. "Why do you ask? Are you going to write that down?"

"No, I was just curious."

"Well, as much as I miss scones and crumpets, I've found other . . . attractions here." He put his arm around me then, and moved a little closer on the stone.

"Like tofu burgers?" I teased him.

"Like you." Then, to my amazement, he leaned over and kissed me! It happened so fast, I hardly had time to record my impressions. I just remember thinking that Simon's lips were incredibly soft, and his breath felt warm on my ear when he pulled me close. I automatically wrapped my arms around his neck and his heart was thumping so loud, I could hear it.

He kissed me a couple of times, and then very gently laid his cheek against mine. We sat that way for a long time, watching the river and the sunset, and I remember thinking what a perfect moment it was. Another thought crossed my mind, and I started to smile. The river, the sunset, Simon's warm kisses — what a fantastic opening for chapter three!

"I love it!" Sharon said Monday afternoon. We had gone out for pizza after school and were sitting in a back booth at Luigi's, with my notes spread out in front of us. "You've got some really great material here, Amy."

"Thanks," I said casually. "I thought so, too."

"I have to admit you had me worried for a while there."

"Why's that?" I was finishing up the last of my chocolate soda, and debating whether or not to have another piece of pizza.

"Well, you have to admit you got off to a slow start," she said archly. "Jogging, picnics, not even a lousy kiss," she added, flipping through my notebook. "It wasn't exactly great romance material."

"I'm a slow starter," I said defensively.

"Well, you more than made up for it," she said generously. "I love this part about the sunset and the river. I think we'll have to put it in chapter three," she said, consulting her outline. "Chapter two is already pretty full."

"Okay," I said agreeably, then did a double take. Sam Collins was heading straight for the booth next to ours. He was wearing a white tennis sweater with white shorts, and had a terrific-looking blonde with him.

As he slid into the booth he spotted me, and nodded politely. "Hi there, Amy."

"Hi, Sam," I said as Sharon's head shot up. "How's your game?" The last time we had played tennis, Sam had volleyed the ball right out of the court.

"It's getting better," he laughed. "Lisa's a great teacher." He smiled at the blonde, who was staring vacantly into space. He nudged her and she reluctantly turned her attention to us. "Amy and I used to play together," he explained. "Tennis, I mean," he added quickly.

"Oh." Lisa yawned and gave me a bored look. A conversational genius she wasn't.

The waitress came to take their order then, and I noticed Sharon watching me suspiciously. "Hah! Some teacher she'd be," she sniffed. "How could he dump someone like you for someone like her?"

"Sharon, it's okay, really." I smiled at her loyalty. "In case you haven't noticed, I am totally, one-hundred percent over my crush on him."

She stared at me. "You are, aren't you?" she said finally. "Do you think it was the book that did it?"

"I guess so," I nodded. "It's certainly given me a lot to think about these past couple of weeks. So that must be it." Of course it was the book that was responsible, I thought, as Sharon bent over my notes. Unless . . . there was a nagging thought nibbling at the edges of my mind, but I resolutely pushed it away.

The book had saved me. There was no doubt about it.

Sharon and I decided to work at her house for a couple of hours after dinner, and were sitting in her immaculate room when her mother knocked lightly on the door. She was wearing a fawn-colored suit with a white blouse and looked very elegant.

"How's the book coming, Amy?" she said cheerfully.

"Fine, Dr. Blakely," I said.

"It's certainly cured Amy of her crushes,

Mom." Sharon smiled at me. "She saw her ex-boyfriend with another girl today, and she didn't even flinch."

"That really is progress. It looks like writing a book paid off for you, didn't it, Amy? And who knows, maybe you've started a whole new career for yourself."

"Uh, I don't think so," I said, looking at the papers spread all over the bed. "It's taken us a couple of weeks just to outline the first few chapters."

"But I think it will go a lot quicker once Amy starts on the actual writing," Sharon piped up.

"I hope so," I admitted. "I can just see myself in twenty years, still stuck on chapter three."

"That will never happen," Dr. Blakely laughed. She tossed a light beige cape over her shoulders and checked her watch. "I'm going to a meeting, Sharon, so don't stay up too late, okay?"

"I won't," Sharon said dutifully. I knew she wouldn't either.

When her mother left, Sharon turned to me. "Maybe you should set some sort of deadline for yourself. The writing might go a lot faster if you had a goal in mind."

"Hmmm," I said, not thrilled over the idea. Although I had to admit Sharon was probably right. She's always reading time management books, and once she even divided her day into fifteen-minute intervals. She always says that if you can't account for your time, you're probably wasting hours, and I suppose she's got a point.

"You can't just wait for inspiration to strike," she persisted. "A lot of writers force themselves to write a certain number of pages every day. Mrs. Harding said so."

"All right, Sharon," I said, relenting. "I'll start doing half a chapter a day, how's that?"

"That's great," she said enthusiastically. She pulled out a pocket calendar and started marking it.

"What are you doing?" I asked, curious.

"I'm figuring out how long it will take you to do the book," she said surprised. "When's your next date with Simon?"

"Next Saturday. We're going dancing."

"Dancing!" she exclaimed. "That's perfect." She frowned and made some rapid scribbles in her book. "Today's Monday, so if you do a half a chapter a day, you'll be up to chapter three on Saturday. . . ."

"And?" I questioned.

"And that's just when we run out of material. We have enough for three chapters, remember? So the timing is great — you'll be all set for another installment with Simon. And we could use a dancing scene in the book. I didn't really want to do anything else with jogging, did you?"

"No, I guess not," I said thoughtfully.

"The dancing scene can be the beginning of chapter four." She clapped her hands together. "I can't believe how perfectly everything is working out, Amy. We've got enough material for three fantastic chapters. We've got a terrific hero and heroine, a great plot, and some wonderful settings."

"It sounds like you've thought of everything," I said wryly.

"Well, I certainly hope so," she said, brightly. "We've got all the raw material for a dynamite book. Now all you have to do is write it!"

Thirteen

I was amazed at how fast news of my book spread through school the following week. Every day half a dozen girls would corner me between classes, each dying to tell me all about her love life. I had just finished listening to a particularly boring tale about Ashley Boyle's romance with a camp counselor when I bumped into Sharon, who was sprinting madly down the corridor. She had just come over from gym class, and for once her sleek golden hair was a mass of tangles.

"What's the rush?" I said as she nearly bowled me over.

"I'll explain in a minute; but quick, let's duck into study hall," she said. "Karen Clover is hot on my trail with material for chapter five."

"You think you've got problems," I said quickly, when we were settled in the back row. "I just listened to Ashley Boyle tell me how she fell in love with the lifeguard at Camp Winnetonka last summer."

"I know all about it," Sharon said with a shudder. "She got me this morning with the same story." She opened her loose-leaf notebook and traced a magenta fingernail across the page. "I first noticed Bud's Australian crawl," she read in a sing-song voice. "I loved everything about him, his arms, his legs, even the golden hairs on his hands. . . ."

"He had hair on his hands?" I giggled, and the monitor at the front of the room motioned me to be quiet.

Sharon started laughing then, too, and pretended to blow her nose until she could get herself under control. "Yeah, he sounds like a werewolf," she kidded.

"I've never seen a blond werewolf," I said innocently, and that sent her into gales of giggles again.

"What are we going to do with all this stuff?" she said a moment later, wiping her eyes. "You wouldn't believe how much material I've collected . . ." she flipped through the notebook, shaking her head sadly ". . . or how awful most of it is."

"Well, we don't have to use all of it. After all, the main plot will be about Simon," I said thoughtfully. "But I suppose everyone will be hurt if I don't use at least a few of the stories they've told me."

"They'll be very hurt," Sharon agreed. "You'll have to have some sub-plots, and bring in as much of this stuff as you can."

"I'll try," I promised her.

Later that night, I sat at my desk, lost in a sea of paper. I had two notebooks crammed with material — Sharon's and my own — plus bits of dialogue I had been scribbling down on my dates with Simon.

Simon. He had been such a lucky choice, I mused. He was funny, and cute, and the fact that he was English would add a whole new dimension to the book. So would the fact that he was a vegetarian, I decided, looking at my notes on tofu. There was something comical about the white squiggly food, and a tofu scene would add a lot of humor to the book! I could hardly wait to capture everything on paper.

How to put it all together? I wondered. I put a fresh piece of paper in the typewriter, and felt a little shiver of excitement.

Chapter One.

The words looked stark, centered neatly on the snowy page. How should I open the book, with description or dialogue? I struggled for a good opening line, and then remembered the first time I had seen Simon. He had been leaning against a tree outside the gym, wearing a blue denim work shirt with the sleeves rolled up. It was very bright out, I remembered, and he was wearing a pair of silver aviator sunglasses.

Tentatively, I started to type.

"Honey, it's nearly eleven," my mother said, hours later. I had been working steadily, reliving moments with Simon, and blinked foggily at her.

"I guess I got so wrapped up, I lost track of time," I apologized. My mother firmly believes that growing girls need eight hours sleep, even though she's a night owl herself.

"That must be a fascinating assignment," she said, looking at the stack of neatly typed pages.

"It's my first novel," I said proudly. I couldn't believe how much progress I had made. All the little scraps of dialogue had been woven into a strong, romantic scene between the hero, Sean Anderson, and the heroine, Melissa Crane.

"You're really serious about this," my mother said, surprised. "I was afraid that writing a novel was just another of your passing fancies." My mother knew that some of my grand passions disappeared in half a day. "Did you stick to the idea of a romance novel?"

"Oh, yes," I said seriously. "It's the only kind of book I feel qualified to write."

She chuckled at that, but I didn't mind. "Well, everybody needs a little romance in her life. I remember when I first met your father, I tried to encourage him to be more romantic."

"You did?" I had always wondered how my parents managed to get together since their personalities are so completely different.

"I wasn't very successful," she admitted ruefully. "He's just not the type to remember birthdays and anniversaries, or send flowers and candy."

"Did you try dropping some hints?" I asked, curious.

"Did I ever!" She ran a hand through her thick chestnut hair and laughed. "I even signed his name to valentine cards and sent them to myself! Talk about drastic measures. . . ." She shrugged and smiled at me. "I hope the boy in the book is a real romantic," she said.

"Oh he is," I assured her. "Very romantic."

She said good-night then, but I went back to the typewriter. Determined to turn out a few more pages, I typed steadily for the next hour and a half.

"You're already on chapter two?" Sharon said delightedly the next morning. "At the rate you're going, you'll be turning out dozens of books!" We were chatting in the hall for a few minutes between classes.

"I don't think so," I said sleepily. "Writing takes a lot more out of you than you think," I said wryly. The truth was, I hadn't gotten to sleep till three, and I felt more dead than alive.

"Well, it's worth it," Sharon insisted. "After all, not everyone has the talent for writing like you do. It would be a shame not to use it. Just think, you'll be a famous author someday!"

"Who's going to be a famous author?" a

low English voice said, and Sharon and I both jumped.

"Uh . . . Amy is," Sharon blurted out.

"You are?" Simon looked a little suspicious, and I knew I had to come up with something fast.

"Sharon thinks I'm going to be an ace reporter someday. Because of my work on the school paper." I laughed, and gave him a you-know-what-friends-are-like look.

"Yeah, and I'll tell everyone I knew her when she was a nobody," Sharon piped up. Hardly the most tactful remark in the world, but I was too jittery to care.

Simon smiled. "She'll never be a nobody," he said, swinging an arm around my shoulders. I saw Sharon make an okay sign to me out of the corner of my eye, and I hurriedly pulled Simon down the hall.

"Was I taking you away from anything important?" he said in that low, husky voice I had described so well in chapter one.

"No, Sharon and I were just — " I stopped, flustered. "We were just talking about things, but it's nothing that we can't . . . uh, discuss later." I was babbling like an idiot, but it couldn't be helped. Simon had an amused look on his face, and I could feel my cheeks flaming.

I was going to say something to remedy the situation, when he squeezed my hand. "You're a funny girl, Amy," he said, as we made our way down the hall.

"Funny, how?" I wasn't sure I'd like what he had to say, but I was curious.

"Oh, you're so open sometimes, and so mysterious at others. . . . It's hard to know what you're really thinking."

"Mysterious? Nope, no way," I assured him. The bell rang then, and Simon and I paused. He was heading toward physics, and I was going in the opposite direction, to geometry class.

"Are you sure about that?" he said, playfully chucking me under the chin.

"I'm positive," I teased him. "In fact, you could say . . . I'm an open book!" I couldn't resist the pun.

"Till Saturday then," he said softly, and vanished around the corner.

I spent the next few days working frantically on the first three chapters, so I would be "caught up" for my Saturday night date with Simon.

We were going to a new disco that had just opened, and I was really looking forward to the evening. I had agonized over what to wear, and had finally decided on a yellow mini-dress with a red braided belt and red flats.

Simon obviously approved, because he let out a low whistle when I met him at the door.

"You look fantastic," he said, and surprized me by leaning over and kissing me lightly on the cheek. "I love your hair that way." He touched a strand that had escaped from my barrette, and let his hand linger briefly on my neck.

"I'm glad," I said a little unsteadily. There was something about Simon's touch that was . . . what? I frowned, groping for a word. *Electrifying*, that was it, I decided. Whenever Simon touched me, I felt a jolt that went all the way down to my toes! I didn't dare whip out a notebook though, so I reminded myself to jot it down when I got home.

"What are you smiling about?" Simon asked after we had gotten into his car.

"I'm just happy," I answered truthfully. "It's a beautiful night, and I'm going to an exciting new place."

"You didn't mention your date," he said in mock reproach.

"With the world's most terrific boy," I kidded him.

"That's better," he said firmly. He leaned over and kissed me lightly before starting the engine.

Carmichael's was a place where people go to dance, and to be seen, and we had no sooner walked in the front door then we bumped into a group of kids from school.

"Hey, Amy, wanna sit with us?" Lucy Skinner's voice boomed across the room. She had tried for the rock-star look, with a lacy hot pink blouse, fluorescent rubber bracelets, and shocking pink heels.

"What in the world is that?" Simon whispered, and I had to smother a giggle.

"That is Lucy Skinner," I explained.

"What's she done to herself?" he said in amazement.

I had to laugh. "I guess that's her disco look." A quick glance at the crowded dance floor proved that the costume look was big — most of the girls were sporting mesh tops, textured hose, and enough bangles to outfit Mr. T. Even Karen Clover tottered by in three-inch purple spikes and a slinky white tank dress, while her friend Shirley Hill boogied in a skintight Hawaiian-print jumpsuit.

I looked at my bright yellow mini-dress and suddenly felt uncomfortable. "I look like I'm going to my grade-school graduation," I muttered to Simon, who laughed and pulled me onto the dance floor.

"You're fishing for compliments," he breathed into my ear. "You know darn well you're the best-looking girl here."

I stared at him, waiting for a wink or smile, but he looked at me steadily. "You really mean it," I said, astonished.

"Of course I do," he said huskily. He pulled me close as the pulsating sounds of Duran Duran filled the room. "I thought you were beautiful the first day I met you outside the gym."

"I can't believe you remember that far back," I said, trying for a light tone.

"I sure do. I even remember what you were wearing," he said, staring down at me. The strobe lights were making interesting shadows on the strong planes of his face, and his eyes were very intense. "A yellow blouse, jeans, and this gold necklace." He fingered the gold chain around my neck.

"You . . . uh, must have a photographic mind," I said uncomfortably. Things were moving a little too fast for me, and I wondered how to put on the brakes.

"Only when something really captures my attention," he retorted, and wrapped both arms around my waist. We swayed to the music for a while then, while my heart did a peculiar little flip-flop in my chest. I'll have to remember everything about this moment, I thought, trying to focus my attention on the dance floor. Somehow, I'll have to capture it all — the strobes, the throbbing music, Simon's warm arms around me — and write it down the minute I get home!

"This is just the beginning, you know," Simon breathed into my ear.

The beginning of another chapter, I almost said aloud. We were standing with our arms around each other on the front porch, and for once, Matthew was nowhere in sight.

"The beginning?" I said, even though I knew what Simon meant.

"For us," he said seriously. "We're going to have lots of good times together." He rubbed my back very gently, and I could feel myself relaxing against him. "We're going to go dancing a lot, and jogging a lot, and play tennis a lot. . . ."

"Do you do everything a lot?" I teased him.

"I sure do. Especially this." Then he kissed me two or three times, while I snuggled against him. I was just thinking what a terrific way he had of kissing — and how to describe it in my book — when someone slammed a car door, and we both jumped.

"Right on cue," Simon muttered, pulling back. "Your brother has an uncanny sense of timing."

"Hi, Matthew," I said, without turning around.

"Oh, hi Simon," he said, ignoring me. He bounded into the house then, and Simon and I looked at each other.

"I guess it's getting late, anyway," Simon said reluctantly. He traced my cheekbone with his finger and said softly, "Can I see you tomorrow? There's a concert in the park — "

"Oh, I can't tomorrow, Simon," I said quickly. "I've got a project to finish."

"It won't take all day, will it?" he pleaded. "We could go out for brunch. I promise to have you back early."

I shook my head. "No, I really need to spend the whole day working." I wanted to finish chapter four and get a good start on chapter five.

He started to say something, then sighed and smiled at me. "Okay, I won't press you. But you'll have to make it up to me next weekend, okay?" He kissed me on the cheek and disappeared down the steps before I had a chance to answer.

Fourteen

"The author's hard at work," I heard Mom saying to Sharon. It was a drizzly Sunday afternoon, and I had been typing steadily all day.

Sharon tapped lightly on the door to my room. "Your collaborator's here," she yelled cheerfully. She swept in so fast she nearly tripped over a pile of bond paper I had stashed by the desk. She opened her mouth to say something, but I held up my hand. "Okay, I won't say a word. Creative disorder." She sighed and moved a mountain of books off the armchair.

I could hear her tapping her long fingernails impatiently on the edge of the desk, but I finished typing a line of dialogue before looking up. "Hi, Sharon," I said, stifling a giant yawn. "What time is it, anyway?"

"Time to take a break," she said promptly. "Why don't we run into town and splurge at

Temptations? Wouldn't you just love a hot fudge sundae right now?"

"I would, but — "

"I know, you have another chapter to go." She flung herself out of the chair and crossed restlessly to the window, staring at the flat gray sky. "Honestly, Amy, they're going to put that on your tombstone." She folded her arms over her chest dramatically. "Here lies Amy Miller, romance novelist. She only had one more chapter to go." She paused and stared at me. "I hate to say it, but you're not much fun anymore."

"Hey, you're the one who's been cracking the whip," I said mildly. "I would have been content to just plod along, writing a few lines a day, but you decided that I needed to turn out half a chapter."

"I know," she said, carefully smoothing her pastel linen pants before she sat down again. "It's all my fault. I created a monster."

"No," I kidded her, "you created an author."

I looked back at the typewriter, and was surprised to find that the words were a blurry smudge across the page. Maybe Sharon was right. I'd been at this too long. It wouldn't hurt to take a short break, I decided. I pushed my chair back, and stretched my arms over my head. "I got a good scene out of Carmichael's last night," I said casually. "Lots of dancing and kissing, just like you ordered."

"Right on." She flipped her gleaming blonde

hair over her shoulder, gave a small self-satisfied smile, like a cat. "That's what romance books are made of." She inspected her nails and then said lightly, "Simon still doesn't suspect a thing, does he?"

"No, I'm sure he doesn't. I don't take notes anymore, you know. That was getting to be a little too obvious." I flushed, remembering my "leaf book," and my pretended fascination by the botany in Ridley Park. "I just rely on my memory now, and try to reconstruct the dialogue and setting as best I can when I get home. I think it's turned out much better than I expected."

"Well, when do I get a peek at it?" Sharon said with a funny little laugh. "I'm beginning to think you're going to keep your manuscript under wraps forever." She grinned, to show she was kidding, but I thought I noticed a flicker of annoyance in those cool blue eyes.

"As a matter of fact," I said lightly, "tomorrow's the big day. I talked to Mrs. Harding on Friday, and she said she'd devote half of English lit. to a reading."

"A reading?" Sharon gasped. "Then it's true? You're going to read it to the whole class?"

"Not only our class. She's invited two more sections to come if they want. I'll be reading the three chapters, and then there'll be a question and answer period."

"Wow," Sharon said, for once at a loss for words. "Well, what about . . ." she bit her lower lip nervously ". . . a sneak preview? You're not going to keep me in suspense until tomorrow, are you?"

"Sorry, it's not in finished form yet." That wasn't exactly true, but it was the first excuse I could think of.

"I don't mind reading a rough draft," she persisted desperately. "After all, I am the collaborator."

Was that what she was afraid of? I wondered. That I wouldn't give her any credit for the book?

"Of course you are," I said soothingly. "And that's going to be the first thing I mention in class tomorrow morning. Without you and your parents, there wouldn't even be a book, remember?"

She smiled happily. "That's true," she said earnestly. "You'd still be loading up on cupcakes, and pining over Sam Collins."

Sam Collins! I had completely forgotten about him. It was amazing how many changes had happened in the past few weeks. Sam Collins belonged to another lifetime.

"You're sure I can't have just a peek?" Sharon pleaded half an hour later, as she was getting ready to leave. "I don't care what sort of form it's in."

"But I do," I said quickly. "I want you to see the book at its best, Sharon. And anyway, you already know the plot."

"Right," she agreed. "We worked together on the outline," she reminded me.

"And I followed it exactly," I assured her.

"Don't worry, there won't be any surprises tomorrow."

"It's not often we have an author visit our class," Mrs. Harding was saying the following morning. A few kids looked at the door, as if expecting a fascinating guest to materialize at any minute. "And to think that we have an author right here in our own midst. Well, that's just the icing on the cake, isn't it." Mrs. Hastings laughed at her own joke, while I caught myself wincing at the image. Icing on the cake? If one of us had written that on an essay, she would have blue-penciled it, with a stern warning not to be trite scribbled in the margin.

I sat hunched over in the first row, willing myself to be calm. I'm always a bundle of nerves when I have to speak in front of the class, and this time was no different. My mouth was dry, my pulse was racing, and my heart was doing a peculiar little rain dance in my chest. I felt like I was about two minutes away from death.

I glanced around the crowded classroom, surprised at the number of kids that had shown up. Sharon was sitting right behind me in the second row, and Karen Clover and Shirley Hill were huddled beside her. Lucy Skinner was smirking from a corner, probably convinced that the whole first chapter was devoted to her love life. Ashley Boyle caught me staring and winked broadly, as if the two of us were in on an exciting secret. I smiled and nodded, wondering how she'd feel when she discovered that her summer romance was reduced to half a page in chapter two.

All at once, there was a surprised gasp from the room, and I realized that Mrs. Harding had introduced me. The moment of truth had arrived, and my knees were so wobbly, I didn't see how they could possibly carry me to the podium.

Sharon gave me a rough jab in the back, there was a smattering of snickers and applause, and suddenly I was facing the class. Fighting an urge to turn tail and run, I gripped the podium with slippery hands, and shuffled my papers.

I opened my mouth once to speak, but nothing came out, and I closed it abruptly. Mrs. Harding must have realized what was happening, because she rushed to fill in the gap.

"Don't be nervous, Amy," she said cheerfully. "You're among friends, and we're all very excited to hear what you have to say."

I saw Oscar Carson leering at me from the third row, and my spirits sagged. Knowing Oscar, he'd be laughing like a hyena before the hour was up.

"Uh, I'd like to read you the first three chapters of my new book," I said hesitantly. "It's a romance novel . . ." this news was punctuated by a giant guffaw from Oscar ". . . called *Love on the Run*, and it's about

146

two teenagers who meet and fall in love while jogging."

I noticed that Karen, Shirley, and Lucy were sitting on the edge of their seats, all with identical grins on their faces. Probably each one thinks she's Melissa, I thought idly, my eyes running down the page. I took a deep breath and began to read.

"Melissa Crane shook her long blonde mane, and shivered inside her bright Mexican poncho as she approached the schoolyard. It was a crisp November day, and the flat gray sky held the promise of snow." Oscar Carson yawned extravagantly, but I ignored him and continued. "As far as Melissa was concerned, it was a day like any other, and she had no way of knowing that in the next few minutes something momentous would happen — something that would change her life forever."

I took another breath, pleased that I had my voice under control. The reading was going better than I had expected.

The next ten minutes passed quickly, and I was well into chapter two when I knew that something was wrong. The room was suddenly still, except for a few whispers coming from the second row. What in the world was going on?

"Melissa's childhood wasn't an easy one," I said, trying to put a lot of expression in my voice. "Her parents were both psychiatrists, and both of them analyzed her endlessly. There were times when she felt more like a patient, than a daughter. They both had offices in their home, and when Melissa was a little girl, she used to play with the skull her father kept on his desk." I couldn't see Sharon's reaction, because Harriet Brody's head was in the way, but I knew she'd get a kick out of the part about the skull.

I went back to my reading, and before I knew it, I was deep into chapter three. This was my favorite part of the book, where Melissa realizes she is falling hopelessly in love with Sean.

"She was attracted by his voice — low and husky with a charming English accent. In fact, she loved everything about him. His rugged good looks, his sense of humor, his playfulness. The two of them were remarkably alike, she decided, except for one thing: She knew she'd never share his passion for tofu."

"Simon Adams," somebody said loudly in the back row. This was followed by a chorus of giggles. "She's talking about Simon," a tall boy wearing a basketball jersey said. "He's the only kid in school who eats tofu."

I read on, trying to look unconcerned. "When he touched her hand, it was like a jolt of electricity shooting up her arm — was it the same for him? A look at his flashing eyes and intense expression told her it was."

And now, the inevitable triangle. "But what could he do about Trudy Phillips?" I said tragically. "He had asked her to go steady just the week before, he'd promised to love her forever. Not that Trudy, with her frizzy, orange hair, was any match for the beautiful Melissa. But Sean didn't want to hurt her. . . ." I read steadily for the next ten minutes, and when I finished chapter three, I lowered my eyes modestly and waited for the applause.

There wasn't any. I counted to ten, wondering why the room was eerily silent, when Mrs. Harding cleared her throat nervously.

"Well, that was certainly interesting, Amy." She sounded a little too enthusiastic, and I knew something was wrong. "I'm sure everyone has dozens of questions for you, so why don't we spend the last five minutes in class discussion? Just feel free to jump in, everybody."

Karen Clover didn't need any encouragement. "I've got a question, all right!" she yelled. She was so angry, she was practically bouncing off her seat in the front row. "Who do you think you are, Amy Miller? You've got a heck of a nerve!"

I licked my lips and smiled nervously. This wasn't the kind of class discussion I had in mind. What was she getting at? "I really don't see — " I began.

"Don't give me that —," she paused and glanced at Mrs. Harding — "garbage." She glared at me. "Look, Amy, you made fun of half the people in this room in that stupid book of yours. Isn't that right, girls?" She looked at Lucy Skinner and Shirley Hill who nodded earnestly.

"Karen!" Mrs. Harding sounded shocked. "I'm sure Amy didn't mean to hurt anyone's feelings."

"You're wrong, Mrs. Harding. I think she enjoyed every minute of it," Karen went on relentlessly. I wanted to shrivel up and hide like a hermit crab, as her voice ricocheted around the room. "I think she had a great time, asking everybody for details of their love lives, and then turning them into funny one-liners."

I could feel my palms getting sweaty as I gripped the podium. "Karen," I said as patiently as I could, "aren't you forgetting something? Everyone *wanted* to be included in the book. In fact, you and Lucy and Shirley practically *insisted* that I use everything you told me." I looked desperately at Sharon for corroboration, but she gave me a cold stare. No help from that quarter. "I thought I was doing all of you a favor," I said lamely.

"A favor!" Ashley Boyle's voice boomed from the back row. "Do you think I enjoyed hearing my boyfriend described as a werewolf?"

There were a few snickers from the back row and I winced, remembering Bud, the lifeguard with the hairy hands. It was a cheap shot, I suppose, but it had gotten a laugh.

"And what about the scene at the wienie

roast?!" Karen demanded. "You took everything I told you about Roger Erdman and twisted it around. Anything goes when you want to make a joke, doesn't it?" Karen's lip quivered, and I wondered for an awful moment if she was going to cry. "I never would have told you he spilled an ice cream cone down my blouse, if I'd known it would turn up in chapter two!"

"And don't forget the way she described us," Lucy Skinner said, getting in on the act. "Did you really have to say that Karen's hair reminded you of a orange tabby cat?"

"Karen wasn't even in the book," I hedged. Actually, this was a fib. In chapter one, Trudy Phillips insisted her hair was "spun gold," even though it looked more like an orange brillo pad. I had lifted that whole line from a lunchtime conversation with Karen.

"Don't lie to us," Shirley Hill said quietly. "You said that I looked like a giant avocado in my green jumpsuit and that Lucy had shoulders like a linebacker. You'll do anything for a joke, won't you? You don't care who you hurt! It's bad enough you insulted the kids in the class, but you even made fun of your best friend." She stared at Sharon Blakely, who looked like she wanted to drop through the floor. "I suppose it's just a coincidence that both of Melissa's parents are shrinks, right?" she said cuttingly.

"Yeah, and I guess it was just a coincidence that Sean Anderson eats tofu!"

Oscar Carson chortled. "No resemblance to anyone living or dead, right?"

The laughter rose like a wave around me, and I could feel my cheeks burning. Mrs. Harding tried to intercede, but it was too late. "Please, everyone," she said, fluttering her hands and rushing to the front of the room. "Let's calm down and have a reasonable discussion about this."

"I don't want to calm down!" Shirley said savagely. The bell rang and she jumped up, clutching her books to her chest. "I just want you to know that I think you're a first-class creep, Amy Miller!"

"Yeah, you may have written a book," Lucy Skinner hissed, "but you've lost a whole bunch of friends."

Everybody filed out on that sour note, and I could feel my knees trembling. To my horror, tears started to well up in my eyes, and I knew if I didn't get out fast, they'd spill down my cheeks. Dimly, I heard Mrs. Harding call my name, but I bolted and tried to dart out the door.

"Hey, can I have your autograph?" Oscar Carson blocked my path with a big grin on his face.

I pushed him aside and ran down the hall, nearly knocking over a couple of freshmen who stared at me in amazement. I kept running until I got to the girls' room, where I locked the door after me, and leaned my head against the cool tiles. I probably imagined it, but I was sure I could still hear the sound of Oscar Carson's cruel laugh ringing in my ears.

"I can't believe you did this to me!" Sharon wailed half an hour later. I had forced myself to call her the minute I got home, half afraid that she would hang up on me. To my relief, she didn't hang up, but she was furious. "I thought you were my friend!"

"I am your friend," I insisted. I decided to bluff my way through. "And what did I do that was so terrible?"

"What did you do!" Her voice was cold as ice. "You made me sound like an absolute idiot in front of the whole class . . . and not only that, you insulted my parents!"

"Insulted your — " I stopped, suddenly understanding. I knew I should have skipped the line about the skull. Sharon and I had seen a plastic skull pencil-holder in a gag store the week before, and I couldn't resist putting it in the book.

"Now everyone thinks Dad really does have a skull on his desk," she said, sounding close to tears. "Everybody knows Melissa was modeled on me."

"But Melissa has a lot of good qualities, Sharon," I pleaded. "She's blonde and beautiful, just like you."

"She's also an air-head, and she has two crazy shrinks for parents. I never want to talk to you again, Amy Miller." And then she banged the phone in my ear.

I sat for a minute, stunned. I thought

Sharon would have been thrilled to have a character patterned after her — how could I have been so wrong?

I scooted off the bed and flew to the kitchen.

"Mom," I said, "you're not going to believe what's going on with Sharon. She's absolutely — "

I never got to finish the line because Mom interrupted smoothly. "Honey," she said, and her voice was artificially bright, "you've got a visitor waiting for you on the front porch."

"A visitor?" I gulped.

"It's Simon," she said, lowering her voice. "And he looks . . ." she paused dramatically ". . . murderous."

I don't even remember walking to the front porch, except suddenly I was facing Simon. And Mom's estimation had been right.

"How's the famous author?" he said sarcastically. He was leaning against the railing, wearing a tan pullover and jeans.

"You . . . uh, heard about the book," I said, stalling for time.

"Only from about a dozen people," he retorted. "Luckily it was just fiction, wasn't it?" he said icily. "I mean it's not like you based it on real people — people who have feelings and could be hurt."

"I never thought you'd be hurt," I said hesitantly.

"Oh, I love being a celebrity," he said, scowling. "You wouldn't believe the jokes I've heard about tofu. It's a shame you only got a chance to read the first three chapters. I'm sure the rest of the book will be a scream." He moved away from the railing, and stood just inches from me. "There's just one problem, Amy. Your main character is calling it quits."

"Simon, wait!" He tried to pull away, but I grabbed his arm, thinking fast. I couldn't believe what a mess I'd made of things! "We need to talk," I pleaded. "Just give me a few minutes to — "

"To what?" He laughed harshly. "Get some material for another chapter? Forget it. Just like they say in books, Amy, this is the end."

He stormed off the porch, just as Matthew bounded up the steps in his basketball uniform. "Hey," Matthew said angrily, "I just heard that you put me in some dumb book of yours."

"Matthew — "

"Don't deny it. Jeff Connors was in Mrs. Harding's class today, and now all the guys are kidding me about it." He paused for breath. "You did write about me, didn't you?"

"Well, there's a scene in chapter three," I said wearily. "Sean and Melissa are kissing on the front porch — "

"And they're interrupted by a big dumb brother who lumbers up the stairs like a moose! So Jeff wasn't making it up. Thanks a lot, Amy," he said, giving me a disgusted look.

F*ifteen*

"How did I make such a giant mess of things?" I said to my mother a couple of hours later. We had just finished dinner, and Matthew and Dad had gone upstairs to work on a computer project.

"Things certainly didn't turn out like you planned," Mom said sympathetically. "But you shouldn't be so surprised at what happened, you know. In a way, it was very predictable." She poured herself a cup of coffee and stood staring out the kitchen window at the sunset.

"Predictable!" I nearly shouted. "How could anybody predict that my friends would act this way? I thought they'd be thrilled to be in the book."

"Did you really?" She turned and stared at me cooly. "Then how come you never told Simon about your plans?"

She had me on that one. "That was different," I muttered uncomfortably. "I figured Simon would object, because . . . well, because he's Simon."

"Because he likes his privacy, you mean. And what about Sharon? Do you think she was thrilled the way you described her and her parents?"

"I suppose I should have asked her about it," I admitted. "I thought she'd be able to see the humor in the part about the skull." I was beginning to miss Sharon already. We'd talked to each other on the phone every night for the past two years, and it didn't seem possible that we weren't going to be friends anymore.

And Simon. . . . I couldn't get the awful scene on the porch out of my mind. It's funny, but I was just beginning to realize how much he meant to me. I hated the idea of not seeing him again, not hearing his jokes, his laughter. I remembered all the times I had teased him about tofu, and he'd promised to make a convert out of me. Not much chance of that happening now, I thought sadly.

My mother, practical as always, broke into my thoughts. "What are you going to do about it? To set things right, I mean."

I bit my lip and thought for a minute. "I've got absolutely no idea, do you?"

"I've got a great idea," Matthew said, coming into the kitchen. He threw himself into a chair and glared at me. "I think you

157

should print a retraction. Then I can show it to all my friends."

"Are you in the book, too?" Mom said puzzled.

"No, it's just a misunderstanding," I said quickly. "He thinks I called him a moose."

"You did call me a moose. Jeff Connors wrote it down," he said defiantly. "And I'm not going to forget this, Amy." He jumped up, grabbed a quart of milk out of the fridge, and headed back to his room.

"I suppose there's only one thing to do, Amy," Mom said slowly, when he'd left.

"What? Jump off a cliff?"

"No, what I had in mind is even tougher." She smiled and I wondered what she was getting at. "What you'll have to do is . . . confess."

"Confess?"

"They say confession is good for the soul," she teased. "If I were you — and I really wanted to see Simon and Sharon again, I'd throw myself on their mercy."

"You would? I don't think that what I did was so terrible, you know." I still felt a little annoyed that everyone was treating me like a monster. Sharon had known exactly what I was doing with Simon. In fact, she'd encouraged me to use him as "material." She just hadn't liked it when the tables were turned on her.

"You're not a monster. But, don't you think it's silly to let pride stand in the way of friendship? After all, you've known Sharon for years, and as for Simon. . . . Well, let's just say I thought there was something special going on there."

"I guess there was," I said miserably. Past tense. There was nothing going on now, Simon had made it very clear that he never wanted to see me again.

"It's not the end of the world, honey." Mom hugged me briefly and then pulled back to look at me. "Why don't you call him? After all, what do you have to lose?"

Calling Simon was one of the toughest things I ever had to do in my whole life. I dialed his number three times, but chickened out and hung up before it even rang. Finally I gritted my teeth, and held on to the receiver for dear life.

"Hello?" Just hearing his voice made my mouth feel dry, and I took a deep breath.

"Simon, this is Amy." There was such a long pause that I wondered if he was still on the line, but I forced myself to plunge ahead. "I'm really sorry about what happened, and I wish we could get together and talk about it."

A long intake of breath; at least he was still on the line. "I don't think that's such a great idea, Amy. It seems like every time I talk to you lately, I read about it later."

That stung, but I suppose I deserved it. "Simon, I didn't want things to work this way, honest. I know you're really mad at me, and I guess I can't blame you. But can't we just, uh, talk it over?" When he didn't answer, I raced on desperately. "Look, I apologize for what happened. It was a mistake, and I'm really sorry."

"I accept your apology," he said very formally. The tone of his voice hurt more than anything else. It was cool, like we barely knew each other. "I really have to hang up now, Amy. I've got a lot of homework to do."

He hadn't said a word about seeing me again, but I couldn't think of any excuse to keep him on the line. "Uh, sure," I muttered unhappily. "I'll let you go."

There was another long pause, and then the sound of someone gently replacing the receiver.

"So that's that," I said softly, wishing the lump in my throat would go away. I brushed my hand over my eyes, and noticed my mother standing in the doorway.

"No luck?" she said sympathetically. I shook my head, and she walked over and rumpled my hair. "Hey, it's not the end of the world," she said quietly. "Why don't you get a good night's sleep, and things will seem much better in the morning. I can practically guarantee it."

A good night's sleep: Mom's famous cure-all. Except this time, it just didn't work. At two that morning, I thumped my pillow for the forty-seventh time, and finally bunched it under my head. A long day, and an even longer night. No matter how I tried I couldn't find a comfortable position, and I couldn't turn off the movie that played over and over in my mind. Simon's face, tight with rage, telling me, "This is the end." Sharon's high-pitched wail, saying over and over, "I thought you were my friend," like some awful Greek chorus.

I willed them out of my mind, but they scooted right back. And brought with them Shirley Hill, Lucy Skinner, and oh, yes, poor Ashley Boyle, hopelessly in love with a hairy-handed lifeguard.

When would it all stop?

Sharon and I didn't have any classes together the next day, so I spent the entire morning wondering what to say to her. Should I try a joke?

"Hey, Sharon, I'm thinking of doing a sequel to *Love on the Run*, and I came up with a great new scene. How about if your father keeps a whole skeleton in his office instead of just a skull?"

No, that would never work. Maybe an abject apology.

"Sharon, if you don't forgive me, I'll never write another novel. Think what the world would miss."

Everything I thought of seemed too risky. What if she ignored me and walked away? By lunchtime, I was still stumped, and wandered into the cafeteria, lost in thought. I was pushing my tray through the serving line, wondering what new horror the cook had dreamed up, when someone jostled my elbow.

"Sorry," a familiar voice muttered. It was Sharon!

I was as happy as a puppy. "Sharon," I said excitedly, "you're speaking to me!"

"I just said I'm sorry," she said crisply. "It doesn't mean I want to talk to you."

"Oh." I felt crushed again. I blindly picked up a dish and plunked it down on my tray. What did it matter what I ate? My whole world was falling apart!

"You hate fried liver," Sharon said mildly.

"You're right, I do." I grinned and put it back, my spirits soaring like a barometer.

"I wouldn't even mention it," she went on, "but I hate to see food go to waste."

"Oh, I do, too," I said solemnly.

We didn't say anything else until we reached the cashier, and then Sharon said in an off-hand voice, "I suppose you can sit with me, if you like."

"Fine," I said, trying not to smile.

"I did a lot of thinking last night," she said, when we found a quiet table in the corner.

"I know what you mean," I said ruefully. "My mind was churning, too."

"What were you thinking about?" she asked.

I decided to lay it all out. "I was thinking that I made a big mistake, not just with Simon, but with you." I stared blankly at my plate, hoping I could find the right words. "I was so busy writing a book, I lost the two people who are the most important to me."

"What happened with Simon?" she asked, forgetting she was supposed to be miffed.

"Don't you remember — " I began, then stopped suddenly. Of course she didn't remember. Sharon hadn't been there to share one of the worst moments of my life. "He came over to my house yesterday," I began. "I've never seen him so mad. I've never seen *anyone* so mad," I amended. "He thinks I used him, and well, he made it pretty clear he never wants to see me again."

After a moment Sharon said quietly, "I'm as much to blame as you are."

Secretly, I tended to agree with her, but there was no sense in antagonizing her. "Oh, I don't think so," I muttered politely.

"No, I am," she insisted. "It's funny, but until yesterday, I never realized how awful it would be having your whole life spread out for everyone to see. When you started describing Melissa in class, I realized you really were talking about me. I felt so awful and embarrassed, I wanted to run out of the room." She put down her fork, and stared at me, her blue eyes troubled. "I can imagine what Simon's going through," she said softly. "Maybe I could talk to him," she offered. "I could tell him that the whole idea was mine, as much as yours."

"It wouldn't do any good," I said, shaking

my head. "He doesn't blame you, he blames me. After all, no matter what you say, I'm the one who wrote the book."

We both were silent for a moment and then Sharon said shyly, "Well, are we still friends? I didn't mean that stuff I said yesterday."

"I'm glad." I smiled at her. "Of course we're still friends." I guess both of us felt a little embarrassed, because we started talking about school then. I felt a great sense of relief. Sharon and I were friends again! That was something to be grateful for.

Mrs. Harding looked a little upset as we filed in for English lit. later that afternoon. She was standing in front of the podium, nervously wringing her hands.

As soon as the bell rang, she pushed her glasses back on her nose, and said quietly, "I think we need to clear the air. It's obvious that many of you were upset by Amy Miller's remarks yesterday."

She flashed me an apologetic look, but I was too stunned to react. What was going on?

"It seems that some of you took Amy's book personally." She paused to let the words sink in. I glanced behind me, and saw Shirley Hill, Karen Clover, and Ashley Boyle smirking in the back row. "In fact, a few of you have complained that you 'recognized' yourselves in the book."

"We sure did," Ashley Boyle whined. "She made fun of us," she said accusingly.

Mrs. Harding gave a diplomatic smile. "I think it's time we set the record straight. Ashley, I'd like you to step up here for a moment."

"Me?" Ashley looked like she wanted to drop through the floor, but she heaved herself out of the chair and ambled to the front.

"Read this, please." Mrs. Harding handed her a hardcover book, opened to the first page.

Ashley glanced at it and said sullenly, "This book is a work of fiction. Any resemblance to actual persons, living or dead, is purely coincidental."

"Does anybody have any questions?" Mrs. Harding said challengingly. She stared around the room while Ashley slunk back to her seat.

"Amy's book is also a work of fiction," she said, her voice clear and crisp. "Luckily, Amy was nice enough to let me keep her copy overnight, and I'm glad she did, because it gave me the opportunity to check a few things." She adjusted her glasses once more and consulted her notes. "For example, four different people came to me and insisted that they were Sheila in the disco scene, two girls swore that they were Heidi in chapter two, and three students felt that Melissa was modeled on them."

I shot a glance at Sharon, and nearly laughed at the amazed expression on her face.

"Can you see what's happening here, class?

All of you see bits and pieces of yourselves in Amy's work. But what you must realize is that her book isn't modeled on any one of you in particular. Like any writer, her writing is the sum total of everything she's seen and experienced." She smiled warmly at me. "In fact, I'd say it's a credit to her talent, that so many of you seem to see yourselves in the book." She paused, and the room was very quiet. "Is there anything you'd like to say, Amy?"

"Just that I'd like to give credit to my collaborator, Sharon Blakely. Without her cracking the whip, I never would have gotten this far with the book." I grinned at Sharon who gave me a regal nod like Princess Di does in the newsreels. "And if my book has made anyone unhappy, I'm really sorry. I never meant to hurt anybody's feelings, and if it ever gets published, I'm going to dedicate it to the whole English lit. class."

Someone in the back of the room started clapping then, and in seconds, the whole room was cheering. Sharon and I looked at each other in amazement. Everything had suddenly changed for the better!

Well, maybe not quite everything, I thought, as I bounded up the front porch a couple of hours later. The situation with Simon was hopeless, and I felt sad and — it surprised me to realize this — lonely. I hadn't seen him all day at school, and I supposed that he was avoiding me. I could hardly blame him, after everything that had happened, but admitting that didn't make me feel any better.

I was on the top step when I noticed the porch swing creaking. Funny, I thought, I'm the only one who ever sits on it.

When my foot hit the porch, I nearly keeled over backward. Simon was sitting on the swing, rocking slowly back and forth, looking at me with what the romance writers would call "an amused glint in his eye." He was wearing a navy-blue running suit and looked unbelievably handsome.

"Your mother said it was okay if I waited for you," he said casually. He smiled at me, as if we had just parted the best of friends, and patted the cushion beside him. "I saved a seat for you," he offered.

"Uh, thanks," I sat down gingerly and looked at him. "I didn't expect . . . I mean, I didn't think I'd ever see you again."

"I'm sorry about yesterday. I shouldn't have said the things I did," he confessed. "I really lost my temper, and I see now that I was wrong."

I was really confused now and looked at him in surprise. "You do?"

He nodded. "Any similarity to any person, living or dead, is purely coincidental."

I laughed. "You heard what happened in Mrs. Harding's class today."

"I did. And you know something? Now that I've had time to think it over, I realize that she's absolutely right." He reached for my hand and gave it a little squeeze.

I was finding it a little difficult to think straight with Simon sitting so close, and I inched forward, until I was perched on the edge of the swing. "Maybe I shouldn't have written the things I did," I admitted. "It's just that I wanted to write a romance book, and well, you were the perfect subject."

He put his arm around me and edged closer on the swing. "The perfect subject?" he said teasingly. "I guess I should be flattered."

"I suppose my mistake was in not telling you about it," I said quickly. "I really should have let you in on what I was doing, and then you wouldn't have — "

"Wouldn't have reacted like an idiot," Simon finished with a laugh. "I don't know why I got so mad at you, Amy. I should have looked at it as the chance of a lifetime. After all, how many guys get to be the hero of a romance novel?"

"You were a terrific hero," I said softly. His face was just inches from mine, and I had an insane desire to reach out and touch his cheek.

"Really?" he murmured. "Does my low, husky voice really send shivers up and down your spine?" He leaned over and began nuzzling my ear, which was murder on my concentration.

"Absolutely," I gulped.

"And does the touch of my hand send an electrifying jolt up your arm?"

"Always."

"Hmmm," he said, brushing my cheek with his warm lips, "and when I kiss you does it feel like a dozen fiery darts?"

"Did I say that?" I frowned, trying to remember.

"According to my sources that was in chapter two."

"That's a great image," I said seriously.

"You're a great girl." He stopped talking long enough to kiss me very gently on the lips. "How about dinner and a movie on Saturday night?"

"I'd love it," I said breathlessly.

"There's just one condition," he said sternly. "I want you to promise that everything we say and do will be off the record."

I pulled out my notebook, and flipped through it thoughtfully. "Well, it would really be a shame not to get some new material for chapter six," I said, pretending to hesitate. "I need some new settings, and I should tighten up the dialogue a little in chapter five. Oh, and I'd like to bring in one or two new characters — "

"Amy," Simon said threateningly.

He looked so intense, I couldn't tease him anymore. "But I guess just this once, I'll forget about writing. I won't even take notes, if you don't want me to. Look — I'll throw away my notebook, if it will make you feel better." I tossed the notebook over my shoulder and it landed with a dull thud on the doormat.

Simon laughed as he bent to kiss me then, and suddenly all thoughts of settings, characters, and dialogue flew out of my head.

"Remember, from now on, everything is off the record," he said with mock sternness while nuzzling my ear.

"Off the record," I whispered back.

"Do you promise?"

"I promise."

He kissed me again, and I knew it would be a very easy promise to keep.